DIARY OF A MADMAN

MARK YOSHIMOTO NEMCOFF

Glenneyre Press

Los Angeles, CA

ISBN: 1-934602-10-8
ISBN-13: 978-1-934602-10-2

Published by Glenneyre Press, LLC.
Los Angeles, CA
www.wordsushi.com

First Edition

Cover Design by: MYN

FOR ALL OF YOU WHO KNOW YOUR INNER
DEMONS...

BE AFRAID...

ONE

Dear Diary,

Today, I woke up at 7 a.m., stretched for 20 minutes and made myself an egg white and spinach omelet with two pieces of wheat toast and the last of the margarine. Watched the news on KTLA for fifteen minutes. Caught a story about a possible teachers' strike. Afterwards, I took a shower and got dressed (white buttoned-down JC Penney shirt, tan Dockers pants). Grabbed my gym bag and went into the office to pick up some new brochures. Told my supervisor I had a sales call in Torrance, but instead drove three hours to Bakersfield and murdered a man named Phil Testaleone.

Phil's house was located in a tract of small and inelegant homes built in the 1950s. Two bedrooms, one bath, twelve hundred square feet, including one-car garage, all perched atop less than a quarter acre of land. Original brick exterior. Twenty-year-old aluminum windows (why people don't replace those awful things is beyond me?). Roof that appears to have last been shingled more than a decade ago. Chain-link fence in the front. Old picket fence in need of a coat of paint on the south side belonging to the neighbors. Slightly bent screen door (lock already broken). Schlage doorknob lock with two deadbolts on the front and two on the back door leading out into the yard behind the house.

Grass was freshly cut, possibly yesterday (I love that smell). A rusted and forgotten swing set idles near the fence (made back when they used to build them out of steel, and not plastic) right next to a dirty and spider-infested pile of firewood. It was almost 2 p.m. when I got there. I circled the block and saw nobody, which was exactly what I was expecting since in the weeks I had been casing Phil's house nothing in this neighborhood had changed. A few doors down, the one house on the street for sale still had the same sign on the lawn. (And someone please tell me why the hell do realty whores think they need to put their mug shot on everything? Sheesh!).

Three blocks away, I parked on the street with several other cars near the Von's market on Henderson. In the back seat I took the grey meter reader's coverall out of my gym bag and put it on. (It's a bit looser after I dropped those five pounds). The surgical gloves, I slipped into my pocket.

Because there was no need, I didn't bother appearing to be checking meters until I was on Phil's block, and with the hat pulled down on my head and these fake eyeglasses, I was nobody. I once read somewhere that the whole idea when they designed these uniforms was to make the wearer invisible. (I should have thought of getting one of these outfits sooner, but what can you do? Live and learn.)

At Phil's house, I made it into his backyard by hopping over the gate when nobody was looking.

One scary moment, I caught my leg on the top of the fence and slightly ripped the coverall. Quickly checked the fence for fibers and my leg to see if I was bleeding. Luckily no on both, but decided I should seriously consider dropping another five pounds.

With no one home and both neighbors at work, it took me less than a minute to pry one of the flimsy aluminum windows with a screwdriver. As I got it open, I thought of the combined four deadbolts on both doors and had to stifle a small laugh.

I pulled myself into the second bedroom and, once inside, tried to take in the aroma of Phil's house but was denied the home's natural scent by way of a Glade plug-in air freshener trying to convince me summer lilacs smell like something from Dow Chemical.

I'm almost convinced people are so accustomed to what's fake that they prefer it to the real thing. I mean, when the fuck have you ever had grape soda that actually tasted like grapes?

In the hallway, I could catch the hint of bleach in the air and followed it to a pair of accordion doors hiding an old washer/dryer pair. Inside the washer was a load of whites. Hanes underpants and T-shirts, socks. Probably all new, as of two Christmases ago.

The dryer was empty.

Very little in the fridge except for tomato juice, eggs, bread, mayonnaise, mustard, deli-cut lunchmeat (ham and beef tongue) and Swiss cheese. In the cupboards, I found mostly soup and one bottle of imitation maple syrup. There was hardly any doubt in my mind Phil has lived alone here ever since his mother passed away a year and a half ago. Throughout the house, I counted three photos of her. One faded black and white snapshot of a young woman with wavy hair wearing the uniform of a WAC from the Second World War, reminds me of an old postcard.

At some point, I realized I'd been staring at the WAC photo for fifteen minutes. Honestly, it started to give me the creeps, so I pushed it off the wall. After that, I went into the garage to hunt around.

Phil came home right on time, a little past six. I had been waiting just behind the door and when he closed it while flipping through his mail, I grabbed him from behind. I clamped my right hand over his mouth very tightly and used my left to hit him in the neck with the stun gun. He reacted quickly, quicker than I thought, trying to elbow me. Everybody gets one good shot thanks to the adrenaline. Thankfully he didn't get the lucky shot.

His elbow to my ribs didn't hurt at all and as I kicked his legs out from under him and brought him to the floor I could feel the fight go right out of his body. I waited for the stun gun to recharge and hit Phil again, holding it to his skin until he passed out.

I originally had thought I would drag him to the kitchen but after some thought I finally decided on the small dining area.

Phil awoke a half hour later, and as expected, tried to scream through the duct tape covering his mouth. I had wrapped it three times around his head to make sure there was no chance—better safe than sorry. He was secured to a chair at the head of the table, wrists and ankles taped to the thick armrests and legs. They really don't make furniture like that anymore.

I kept the light low and the shades drawn, nothing out of the ordinary. I even put the TV on in the living room. (It's the small details that matter. Remembering them reminds me I'm in control.)

When Phil came to, his eyes went so wide I nearly had to laugh. He looked like one of those old Bugs Bunny cartoons when Elmer Fudd sits on a thumbtack or something. I could see that he was scared, even though he tried to pull it together quickly.

But once he saw what I had taken from his garage, he broke down. He had to have known what was going to happen next.

Truth was, I hadn't expected to find a cordless drill, but I did come across an old plug-in Craftsman that was heavier than a brick along with a nicely coiled twenty-five-foot orange extension cord. The drill bits found in the box nearby were old and needed sharpening, but I was pretty certain they'd be good enough to go through skin, muscle and bone.

Hovering over Phil, I held up the drill and gunned it once for effect. I watched him begin rocking back and forth in the heavy chair, struggling to break free out of instinct. Had he been thinking, he would have realized it was a completely fruitless effort.

Where does the saying "fruitless" come from? Archaic from when folks used to go out foraging to survive and the resulting feeling of coming back empty-handed? I can't understand it. Why not take a crossbow with you? You're bound to find something to eat if you look hard enough.

I let Phil rock back and forth a bit because I could finally smell the acrid scent of sweat coming off him. Eventually, I pushed him backward, tipping him over until he and the chair slammed on the floor half on and half off the Persian rug. I'd bet anything that was a real Persian too, not some made-in-Mexico knockoff.

I leaned down and pushed the point of the bit against Phil's shoulder and the moment I hit the trigger his body jolted as if struck by lightning. I put my other hand on his chest to hold him in place and drilled until I hit bone. I was feeling good so I drilled a second hole before moving to the other shoulder. Then I decided the holes weren't big enough so I went back to the garage. There, hanging on an old pegboard, was a thick, half-inch masonry bit I'd missed before, still wrapped in the blister pack it had been sealed in sometime during the 1970s.

When I'd gotten back to Phil's dining room, he had managed to roll over onto his side in a lame effort to get to the door. I kicked him back over and told him I was going to punish him for his disobedience, and I used the masonry bit on his hip, actually feeling it snap once I punched through the thick bone.

The other thing I'd brought back with me from the garage was a nice old-fashioned claw hammer. I actually had to hold each of his knees down with one hand while I went to work on them with the other. (Five whacks to shatter the left one. Seven for the right.) It had always been my feeling that if you break the knees first, it makes it easier to do the feet without too much of a fight.

I took Phil's shoes off (Florsheim, nice!) but left his socks on (one black, one blue—colorblind, Phil? Maybe?) before using the claw end of the hammer on his feet. Within two or three swings, I'd lacerated them, tearing flesh away with each successive blow. I'd even managed to splatter myself in the process so it was probably a good thing I had on an old apron I found in the kitchen.

Phil squeezed his eyes shut from the pain and it annoyed me so I went through the drawers in the kitchen and found a pair of orange-handled scissors. I put my knee into Phil's chest as I pulled his eyelids up and cut them away. There. The last thing I wanted was to have all this hard work of mine go unappreciated.

I took the scissors in my hand and used one of the points to stab right through Phil's cheek into his mouth where it made a slight popping sound. I kept stabbing his cheek until I'd punched a hole big enough to see his tongue then I began stabbing that as well until it looked like a lump of bloody hamburger. I hadn't been planning on doing that. I love it when I improvise.

Phil had weakened immensely from the blood loss, so I decided to think about wrapping things up a bit. I went into his bedroom to get the items I'd found earlier.

When I showed them to Phil, he began crying and it occurred to me that he hadn't even shed a tear until this very moment. I told him what I like about older gardening shears is that they're made from cold-forged steel. Steel made in the U.S., and not this imported Chinese garbage.

"But I guess you know that by now, huh Phil?" I told him.

When I showed him the cigar box I had found hidden high on a shelf in his closet, he tried to turn away. I opened the lid to reveal all of the tiny severed fingers. Most of them shriveled and blackened with age. One, maybe half the size of my own fingers, looked fairly fresh, maybe a month old.

I held the tiny finger up to him. There was a hint of pink polish on a chipped nail and I thought of a news story I'd seen weeks ago about an eight year-old girl who'd vanished from a playground as her mother's attention was focused on a cell phone. I'd seen the posters with the girl's face as far away as L.A.

Jody Sue Montgomery.

They never found her, and right now I was pretty certain I was holding up her ring finger. One that would never see an engagement or wedding ring because of Phil Testaleone, a forty-seven-year-old pedophile who, as the cigar box would testify, apparently loved to collect trophies.

I put the small and delicate finger back into the box and closed the lid. I picked up the claw hammer and used the head to smash into the duct tape covering his mouth, bringing it down hard as I heard his teeth shatter underneath. I believe I said something to him, but for the life of me, I can't remember what. It'll probably come back to me later.

At some point, I must have turned the hammer around to the claw end because when I looked down, Phil's face had caved in on one side. Quickly, I stopped because I wanted to make sure he was positively identified.

So then I picked up the drill and used the masonry bit on his abdomen and chest, trying to remember where all of the major organs were located. After several tries, I found his heart and sometime during the second hole I'd put in it, it must have given out.

I slipped out of Phil's shirt (and the pair of his shoes I'd squeezed into). In the kitchen sink, I used a lighter to completely melt the surgical gloves I'd been wearing before dropping them down the disposal. I took off my coveralls and put on the dark sweatpants and shirt in my gym bag and left out the back door sometime after 1 a.m. The street was dark and quiet and I walked to my car and drove home. All the way back, I fought the urge to stop and pick up a pack of cigarettes.

TWO

Dear Diary,

At the age of twelve, serial killer Harvey Louis Carignan was placed in a reform school in North Dakota where he was allegedly sexually abused by a female teacher. According to an interview Carignan gave to an author writing a book about his crimes, the teacher would keep him after class and masturbate in front of him and call him names. Any time Harvey tried to touch himself or what he called her "gigantic breasts", she would brutally beat the living shit out of him.

Harvey Louis Carignan would later go on to murder some fifty women. Most of the time with the blunt object that earned him the nickname, "Harv The Hammer".

Maybe it also had something to do with the fact that nearly all of his victims were either vaginally or anally raped with the handle of that aforementioned hand tool.

I'm sure it was a cop that coined that moniker. Most cops have the imagination God gave a toaster.

It's been almost two weeks since my last entry. Sorry. I unexpectedly got called on a sales trip when Jim "Whiney Ass" Maddox got sick again. Luckily, he and I had lunch just last week where he'd told me all about how he intended to promote the new fall line. I had even been in enough of a good mood to pay attention while he was talking—even the parts where he complained about the service, the weather, our boss.

The usual Whiney Ass stuff.

The reason I was feeling so chipper was I had been following the news about our good friend Phil and how the police finally identified several of the contents of his secret trophy box as belonging to a number of missing children going back to 1992. Some, they said, had been too badly decomposed to I.D. One, the newspaper said, even had teeth marks at the point where it had been severed. Apparently, before bringing along his mother's gardening shears, Phil liked to chew his trophies off.

The night before, I said a prayer for all of the children he murdered. There is indeed a special place in Hell for people like Phil Testaleone. One where his screaming will never cease.

On my way to meet Whiny Ass at Olive Garden, I stopped and picked up a sympathy card and mailed it the family of Jody Sue Montgomery. Her mother had been in the paper the day before. I found out where they lived from the article. I hope they don't mind that I didn't sign it.

One other thing I almost forgot about my lunch with Whiney Ass. He was bitching about his ex-wife. I guess she took off with a boatload of stuff he didn't want her to take and now she's asking for more. Apparently, he received a letter from her lawyer saying she wants this big album full of their wedding photos back. In the letter it claimed "she" was the one who picked the photographer, "she" was the one who spent hours putting them into the album. Whiney ass turned to me and said, "Yeah, and she was the one who left. I was the one who wanted to hold onto the marriage. She throws me away and now she wants the photos. No fucking way. And she's not getting the fucking house either."

Poor Whiny Ass. Sometimes I just don't see the point to divorce. It seems like slow death to me.

I saw this somewhere. What has four arms and four legs and never works out?

Marriage.

Whiney Ass was wearing a new white shirt. I know it because he found a pin in his collar while we were sitting there waiting for the waitress. Apparently, it pricked the back of his neck. It was small. Inch and a half with a white ball end.

Of course he bitched endlessly about it while stuffing his face with tortellini.

Regardless (or is it irregardless? I have to look that up), the sales trip went great and I came home with contracts for half a dozen of the PDX-2000s. Apparently, Whiney Ass has been doing his job because when I got to San Diego, those guys were chomping at the bit for them like a bunch of hungry dogs.

All I can say is Whiney Ass picks up the tab next time at the O.G. for all-you-can-eat pasta and breadsticks, because I made sure his clients got a killer deal.

I crack myself up sometimes.

On the drive back from the sales call, I found a breakfast place near Old Town that made the most amazing frittatas (spinach and mushroom, one cup of coffee, two slices of wheat toast, Smuckers grape and apple jelly). As I sat in my booth, I quietly mused over how simple it was to find Phil. In fact, he was the easiest of all of them so far. Maybe I'm getting good at this. Maybe I should have been a cop.

Twenty kids disappear in one county over ten years. Eight turn up as runaways. Twelve of them end up on milk cartons, never to be heard of again. Seven of those snatched in broad daylight during summer months. Two taken from public park bathrooms. Two from playgrounds. Three from shopping malls. One apparently while playing in the front yard while the babysitter was doing laundry. One taken while standing at a school bus stop.

No bodies. No witnesses. Nobody else links these as all related?

Question: How do you "steal" a kid and drive away with no witnesses?

Answer: When you are invisible.

When you blend in so well, you don't draw attention to yourself and nobody remembers you.

When you drive a taxi?

All it took for me was one little mention of the Jody Sue Montgomery story in the paper where the reporter lightly supposed a link in all of the unexplained child disappearances in and around Bakersfield. Just one sentence that seemingly nobody paid attention to.

Except me.

All it took was a few searches on the Internet to find mentions of all of the other missing kids in the area. I dug up all the files I could find on these stories. Not one mention anywhere about police thinking they were related. Truth was, the police didn't seem to care. Nobody did.

Except for one cab driver who started a petition to have the missing kids of Bakersfield put on a billboard, at taxpayers' expense.

I found the two-paragraph story because I'd been obsessively combing the regional news for any mention of any single one of these missing kids. Turns out this one cabbie was asking his customers to sign this petition. He'd shown up at a small candlelit church vigil for a missing 7-year-old named Katie Azarkian. A reporter noticed him and made mention of it. The story made a Tuesday online edition. I waited for a follow-up. There was none.

The cabbie's name: Phil Testaleone.

And to me, the fishy thing wasn't the petition, but that he'd let it die. I took a couple of sick days from work and drove up to Bakersfield. I checked into a motel and called for cabs from the company the article said Phil worked for to take me around. The first day I spent $200 with no luck. Finally, I decided to take a chance and made mention of having seen the article about the cabbie with the petition. The driver told me Phil usually worked Thursdays to Mondays. It was a Wednesday.

The next day, I hit paydirt.

Phil Testaleone was about as average as they come. 5'11", two hundred pounds. He seemed to be taken by surprise when I brought up the story about the petition. I had come prepared. I told him I remembered it because I had a niece that went missing and they never found her. I watched his eyes in the rear-view mirror as I told the fictional version of what her parents went through and how we all believe "Carrie" was tortured. When his irises widened and he swallowed hard, I could see the excitement he was hiding.

If I had looked over the seat, I probably would have seen a big bulge in his pants.

I knew I had my man.

No lie detector can compare to the minute split-second signals you can pick up if you know what buttons to push. In law enforcement, they call it entrapment. Personally, I call it putting fresh meat down where a predator can smell it.

I'd felt the box cutter in my pocket. I could have slit his jugular right there. It took a lot of effort to restrain myself. When it happened, I wanted more time with Phil.

And I liked knowing I had the willpower to stop myself. I have been thinking again about writing a book about emotional strength—helping people quit smoking or eating. I might work on that soon.

I asked Phil what happened to the petition. He said his boss made him stop harassing his customers. I told him if he thought it was important he should still do it. He said he was looking for the time.

He might as well have said that once he'd gotten his name in the paper, he'd accomplished what he wanted. He'd gotten his rocks off, then rolled over and lost interest.

I dug a little deeper. I asked him what there was to do around Bakersfield. His reaction, like any local, was "Nuthin'". After a couple more questions, he offered up, possibly inadvertently, that he'd lived here all his life, knew it inside and out. A quick glance at his left hand yielded no wedding ring.

When I got home, I discovered the obituary about his mother. Thelma Testaleone, aged 86. Loving wife and mother leaving behind one son, Phil. Unlike Phil, she was listed in the phone book. It should have dawned on me sooner why that was—he was staying with her.

In fact, Phil's tax returns that I'd found all pointed to the fact that he had lived at home his whole life.

Except for the few years he spent locked up in a state mental hospital.

I have to thank my buddy Eddy (not his real name) for that one. If I'm nice to Eddy, he hooks me up with files and info you can only get with the kind of job Eddy has. I had mentioned Phil Testaleone's name as the possible Bakersfield Child Killer (my nickname for him, not Eddy's). He called me to tell me about where Phil had spent a few of his teenage years. Phil's juvenile records were sealed, but you don't get sent down to a nuthatch as a kid unless you've set a few fires or got caught torturing a kitten.

This guy had serial killer written all over him.

And not once did I ever find a record of a single cop questioning Phil—probably because those sealed records kept him off anybody's radar. And even if they had given Phil the third degree, there's probably zero chance they would have gotten anything from him.

If it wasn't for me, they never would have found Phil's trophy box on his dining room table—right next to one of the missing child flyers for Jody Sue Montgomery. He'd kept one of those too.

I guess it's true. It takes one to know one.

I doubt a cop could have stopped Phil Testaleone before he killed another child. Hell, a dozen more children.

But I guess that's not an issue anymore.

This has been much easier than I thought it would be, thanks to my buddy Eddy. So far no heat (maybe also thanks to Eddy?) and that's why I finally feel comfortable keeping this journal. I've been careful. As long as I keep changing my M.O., the donut jockeys will never find me and I can keep doing my hobby.

In some countries, they'd probably pay me a fortune to do what I'm doing.

But if I did it for a living, then I'd need a hobby.

And, dear diary, if you haven't guessed, I'm not really the "ship in a bottle" kind of guy.

Strange thing about "Harv The Hammer" Carignan—his victims ranged in age from teenagers to little old biddies he raped and mutilated.

With most of the older women, he bashed their faces in when he was done with them. Smashed their skulls against rocks, concrete floors or with that ever-present hammer until all that was left was a bloody pulp.

But with some of his teenage victims, he would beat them severely but then release them.

On a few occasions, he even drove them home and offered to bandage their wounds. What a fucking guy.

He lusted after the young flesh and despised the old. Every woman he killed represented the Mother, the Grandmother, the Aunts, the Teachers who mistreated him —every domineering and cruel woman.

Because in the state of Minnesota any convict can only serve a maximum of 45 consecutive years behind bars, The Hammer could see the light of day in the year 2021 if he were to live to the ripe old age of 95.

And you can bet, if that happens I'll be there, waiting for him behind a closed door. I'd throw him to the ground, then hold his frail body down with one hand while I used a blade to cut the skin over the top of his head from ear to ear— slice it to the bone, then dig my fingers in and yank it down the way you'd peel an orange.

Then after I tore his face off, I'd stuff it in his mouth and as he choked to death, I'd lean down and whisper the names of all his victims in his ear.

And all this would be before he ever knew what was happening to him. I guarantee it.

This morning I was reading the obits when I came across the following:

Horvath, Gilgamesh Samuel

Gil S. Horvath was born on January 12, 1951. A native of Arcadia, he became a noted filmstrip producer, temple leader and inspiration to his family and friends. Gil produced hundreds of educational programs for schools around the United States through his company, Federated Educational Films, Inc. He was also a talented and prolific composer, often creating all of the original music to go along with his filmstrips. Known to all as a giving man, Gil made a tradition of volunteering at area shelters on Christmas by serving meals to the needy and less fortunate.

I saw that the date for the memorial is this coming Saturday. I'm thinking of going. I'll let you know how it turns out. He sounded like a pretty decent guy, but then again they all do. Nobody puts "cheated on his taxes, drank too much, and hit his wife on occasion" in an obit.

I'll give Gil Horvath the benefit of the doubt on this one.

p.s. twenty-seven days without a cigarette. I think I finally have it licked. Those things can kill you.

THREE

Dear Diary,

The funeral of Gil Horvath, educational filmstrip producer, sometime composer and homeless shelter volunteer, was almost interesting. This is only my second time in a Jewish temple and I almost forgot to put that little hat on top of my head before going in. What is it called? A Yamaha? Yakima?

By the door was a wicker basket that had these chapel prayer booklets with all the usual Jewish funeral psalms 1, 15 and of course the big one, 23, the Valley of the Shadow of Death. But as I'm sitting there paging through it, I notice in the middle of the book is an advertisement for a memorial park and mortuary. An honest-to-God advertisement. Two-page centerfold. I start to understand that it must have been the memorial park that printed up and distributed this chapel prayer book to all the synagogues in the area free of charge.

But an advertisement? Are you fucking kidding me? Are we that crass a society?

Call me crazy but I think by the time the family is seeing this book at the funeral they've probably already picked a cemetery. Do you think they're going to look at this ad with the blue-hued picture of serene trees and well-manicured grounds and go, "Aw fuck, I wish we were burying uncle Morty here! Quick, call the number on the back of the prayer booklet and see what they have available for two o'clock!"

Forty-two people attended the memorial for Gil Horvath including a number of family members. In the men's room, I was fixing my tie and fell into a conversation with Gil's brother-in-law, Isaac, who had hair darker than any other sixty-something-year-old man I've ever seen. (Black two-button blazer. Black slacks, black patent leather shoes—maker unknown, white shirt, grey-and-red-striped tie) He asked how I knew Gil. I told him my cover story, that Gil and I often volunteered at the same shelters serving Christmas dinners to the less fortunate. Isaac seemed less than impressed and grumbled something about Gil being a great man before shuffling away with his fly still open.

I sat in the back of the chapel room and slipped out early. After my encounter with the brother-in-law, I wasn't so sure that my cover story would hold up under more scrutiny.

Better safe than sorry.

Gil died of skin cancer. Melanoma, carcinoma. I don't know, one of the nomas. I've been to the funerals of murder victims, people I've never met, and their relatives are way too suspicious of any unfamiliar faces. I'm never doing that again. Too risky, even if I wasn't involved.

I've never gone to the funeral of someone I've taken. That would be plain stupid.

Today marks thirty-two days without a cigarette. On my way home from Gil's memorial, I started craving a smoke really badly and almost gave in. Instead, I stopped at Borders and sat and read books in the true crime section for three hours until it went away.

You find out some interesting things in bookstores.

I saw an old lady shoplift a paperback romance novel. Slipped it right into her big purse.

I saw a man and wife right in front of me arguing in hushed voices over money. I actually heard him whisper, "You fucking bitch, now I have to go to my brother on my knees again and it's all your fault."

They were two feet away. I just kept my face in the book I'd picked off the shelf and pretended like I was not even there. I was reading about June Stott, a thirty year-old homeless woman living in Rochester who was slightly retarded and extremely shy. She befriended a man named Arthur John Shawcross who occasionally invited her in for dinner.

One afternoon Shawcross saw her sitting on a bench and suggested to Stott that she come fishing with him down by the Genessee River.

At the water's edge, she refused his sexual advances and told Shawcross she was going to go to the cops. He strangled her, then removed her clothes and set them adrift downstream before going home to dinner. A couple of days later he came back, dragged her body into the cattails and used a pocketknife to slice her open from her neck to her anus before pulling out her entrails and tossing them into the water.

Exactly one month later, some dude walking his dog found Stott's body. The police report described her stiff body as having the legs bent at the knee and the buttocks elevated, suggesting the possibility of anal intercourse, post mortem.

Her torso was slashed top to bottom. Her vaginal lips were missing. In a statement made during a prison interview, Arthur John Shawcross claims that he sliced them off and ate them.

On my way home I stopped and picked up a whole rotisserie chicken and a side of steamed vegetables. The girl behind the counter was very nice (blonde hair, brown eyes, maybe 5'2" to 5'3", light acne). I've never seen her before.

It made me think of my sweet little Jennie Bomb. I really miss her. I need to call her this weekend. It's time to make a trip to see her again.

Arthur John Shawcross was convicted in 1991 of the murders of 11 women and one 10-year-old boy. He later claimed most of the women tried to rob him. Nearly all of his victims were street prostitutes. One of them, Darlene

Trippi, was choked to death after she called him hopeless when he couldn't get a boner.

I know I'm nothing like Arthur John Shawcross because I don't have that problem. With my Jennie Bomb, I get so hard you could cut diamonds with my junk. She is not my girlfriend, but one day I'd like her to be. With her, you get the whole GFE (Girlfriend Experience). I do think about her more often than I should.

You know how certain things just seem to be fate? Like when you think of someone and all of a sudden, that person calls you? Not to sound like one of those new age fairy dust-sprinkling mushroomheads, but c'mon, there has to be something to that, some kind of cosmic-flow bullshit thing. It happens more than you know.

It can't all be imagined, can it?

I read about the guy who owned some big brokerage house who called in sick one day because a little voice told him not to go into work. That morning some Arab guys flew a plane through New York into the building he worked in. Everybody in the company died except him.

You think that isn't fate sending you a message?

Then again, maybe he had a golfing buddy in Saudi Arabia who owed him one, who knows? But this kind of thing happens.

On the way back with my chicken (new artwork on bag or am I imagining it?) I thought about calling Eddy to see if he wanted to grab a sixer (domestic only, thank you) and come over, but he must have been reading my mind. When I got home, there was an e-mail from one of the floater accounts he keeps on Yahoo.

Janet Twitty, age 27, mother of one, found dead under a pile of trash in a vacant lot outside of Laughlin, NV. Ligature marks on the hands, ankles and neck indicating victim was tied, possibly hogtied. No rope, however, was found at the scene.

Death came from several blows to the head and multiple stab wounds. Whomever did this beat her and carved her up good. Twitty's left eye socket had been shattered and jaw dislocated. The blade used on her was obviously serrated. Most likely a kitchen knife. Probably a steak knife.

The crime scene photos Eddy has sent show a close up of Janet Twitty's hands. Several broken nails, abraded skin. Signs of a struggle. She was alive while he was carving her up. Her defensive wounds are the kind you get when trying to fend off a blade. Deep cuts in the palms of her hands. Several of them all the way through the ligaments down to the bone.

The report says a rape kit was done. Vaginal trauma was most likely post-mortem and the killer did leave semen.

And a bite mark.

After she was dead, he sunk his teeth into her shoulder, breaking the skin.

According to Eddy, the press hasn't been given this last detail which seems to match perfectly with the M.O. of two other slayings in the area over a one-month period. All the victims were white females in their 20s or 30s. Young mothers and homemakers with no criminal pasts or any known ties to criminal elements.

D.N.A. test results are still at least two weeks away according to Eddy, but it's his guess the semen left behind at all three crime scenes will match up.

He has a suspect though. I can tell by the way he's carefully worded the e-mail. He's asked me if I can make it out to Laughlin any time in the next couple of weeks. I know what he wants from me, and that he'll only tell me more if and when I show up.

I do have a few vacation days saved up. Time is not an issue.

The issue is whether I want to be used like this. Normally, I like to do all of my own legwork. This is the first time Eddy has given me one on a silver platter served up like John the Baptist's decapitated melon.

Is this a trap? Am I being set up?

How much do I trust Eddy?

I have to think about this some more.

Dear Diary,

I slept on it. Eddy has risked quite a bit for me. He has put his ass on the line to give me what he's given me.

And where does that saying come from? I imagine it being quite literal involving a donkey and a roulette table. I mean, "not throwing the baby out with the bathwater" comes from the days when everybody in a family would share a single tub for bathing. The father went first and then the mother and then the children. The last person in line most likely ended up with a cold and filthy bacterial gazpacho and I'm sure someone, at some point, accidentally pitched out a tot by accident when done.

This all feels dirty, but I've decided I'm going to do it. I left a message for Eddy this morning. If I can swing it at work, I can make it out to Laughlin by the end of the week.

Las Vegas is a short drive from Laughlin, which means I can see my little Jennie Bomb. I have to e-mail her to see if she's available. I've been craving the GFE and after Laughlin, I'm going to need it badly. I may treat myself this time to two hours. I want to stay someplace nice this time. Have to look into rooms at the Venetian, Bellagio, Wynn. No more Imperial Palace. Yuck.

I heard they are planning to close down the Grand Tropic. After what happened there earlier this year, I can't blame them. I wouldn't stay there. Besides, I like the places on the Strip. There's something disturbing to me about those backstreet joints, like dirt hidden under the rug.

I will ask Eddy if he wants to join me for a steak dinner. Benihana sounds pretty good to me now. I wonder how long those chefs train with those knives. There has to be a book about it somewhere.

If there is, there's probably a big-ass disclaimer in the front. *Hi, if you slice your fucking thumb off, don't come crying to us, Round-eye, you bought the book. Take some fucking responsibility for your life.*

Or is taking responsibility even the American way anymore? It's getting impossible to tell the cowboys from the Indians.

Thirty-three days without a cigarette.

Dear Diary,

Woke up at 6:45. Stretched for 20 minutes. Did 100 sit-ups, and made an egg white and spinach omelet with two pieces of wheat toast.

News on TV: Teachers still talking strike and now the grocery workers are as well.

Afterwards, I took a shower and got dressed (powder blue buttoned-down JC Penney shirt, gray slacks from Macy's).

When I got into the office, I managed to get Thursday and Friday off, no questions asked. I had a cover story all planned out about a sick relative that I didn't have to use (and will save for a later date). My supervisor, the Lipless Wonder is a complete hamster. It's a pretty loose ship here. How long's that going to last?

No e-mail back yet from my Jennie Bomb. What's up with that? I would die if I couldn't see her. Just in case, I spent an hour at my desk surfing TheEroticReview.com for "independent providers" in Las Vegas. Found over 2,000 of them!

2,000!

Most of them are just real call-girl types, the old in-and-out delivered right to your door. I need more than that. I need the Girlfriend Experience. Found a few other providers that had come very highly recommended by the other hobbyists in the forum including Nikki Avalon, who many says gives the GFE, but appears to be out of my price range. According to everyone's review, she is totally worth it. There was an interesting one named L.J. Montana whose photos I clicked on for over an hour. She sounds like a bit more my speed. My fingers clicked through page after page until I stopped on one that goes by the name of Biscayne. I checked rates. Biscayne sounds like my best bet if my Jennie Bomb can't see me. I will wait until tomorrow. Besides, there's no way I can e-mail Biscayne from here. I'm already taking enough of a chance surfing TER from work. Must be more careful in the future.

Made some calls. Bellagio wanted $450 a night for a room! WTF? Venetian is booked up. I made a reservation at the Flamingo for Friday and Saturday night. They claim the rooms have been redone. I hope so. I'm considering buying one of those

FOUR

Dear Diary,

I've driven through Laughlin a couple of times, even stopped once to get a cheeseburger and take a piss. Neither of those events was actually any more memorable than that. Laughlin is one of those places built on impatience. The whole town is one RCH over the state line and the first place with $5 blackjack and shrimp cocktail. You could fit the whole town into half of a dog's asshole and still have plenty of room for a barn dance.

Even the air, still and pungent with the stink of desperation, feels wrong to me. I see all of these tour busses full of day-tripping oldsters dropping their measly pension checks, sitting at the penny slots with their oxygen tanks and blank stares, and I want to hit somebody. I want to finish this up and get back on the road. I've been thinking about my little Jennie Bomb and our upcoming date on Saturday. I've been dreaming about her a lot the past few days since I know I'm going to see her, touch her... The curve of her hip. The way her breasts fit so nicely in my hands. I don't care that one is slightly smaller than the other.

I want to get this over with as quickly as possible, but I can't get careless.

I also can't do anything until Eddy contacts me with a name and address of the target. I'm checking into a small motel just past town. Gonna shut my eyes and grab some rack time. Gotta put my head on right. Who knows what it may lead to if I can impress Eddy with my professionalism?

Dear Diary,

Eddy sent me a text message at 4 a.m. Drove to a pay phone a mile away to call him back. I love this cloak and dagger shit. I just know I could do this for a living.

His name is Tito Gomez, a Mexican parolee who was released the very day of the first killing. He'd done seven years on a fifteen-to-twenty for the brutal rape of a fifteen year-old girl. Apparently, she had been riding her bike to a friend's house and was walking it across some train tracks near the apartment complex Tito was living in. He followed her and then beat her unconscious with a sixteen-inch long grocery cart handle before raping and sodomizing her then leaving her to die. Several hours later, she crawled back to the road and was able to flag down a passing motorist.

Tito was caught the next day after pawning her bike.

What Eddy told me was that Tito had left a bite mark on the girl's thigh but because the judge had thrown out the photographic evidence based on a technicality involving improper collection of Tito's dental impressions, that particular part of the case was never publicly known. Neither, apparently, was the fact that all of the victims Eddy is linking to Tito had similar bite wounds on various parts of their bodies.

But as Eddy explained, since there was no formal evidence linking Tito to having done such a thing before, the court won't recognize it. And based just on the bite evidence, they couldn't get a warrant to search Tito's home or bring him in for questioning or a dental impression. They have nothing tying him to the case. All they can do is wait for him to slip up.

While he's leaving another dead body behind.

And Eddy doesn't want to give him the chance. Can't say I blame him. The whole thing makes me so angry. What the fuck is wrong with a society that better protects the criminals than the victims?

Tito Gomez is a piece of human waste.

Or should I say: "was"?

He had been working as a dishwasher at the Blue Diamond, one of these corporate-owned McHotels in town (which would give him ample opportunities to obtain a steak knife, but then again who doesn't have a steak knife?). I'd been tipped that he was working the swing shift. Around eleven, I pulled my car onto a side street, a short walk from the employee parking garage. I listened to the radio. In between commercials, they played "We Built This City" by Starship, "China Grove" by the Doobie Brothers, "Owner of a Lonely Heart" by Yes, "My Sister" by Tanya Donnelly, "Basket Case" by Green Day, "Heart Shaped Box" by Nirvana, and "The Way" by Fastball, which I only listened to for a minute or so before heading out with my backpack containing my "kit".

I looked around for video cameras. None found. Most of these joints only care about the security of their guests, so I was not surprised.

A little past midnight, I saw several employees of the Blue Diamond exit out back. Eddy had given me an approximate ID of Tito's car, and I kept my eye on it. And I say approximate, because as it turned out, I was watching the wrong vehicle. It was only by dumb luck that I spotted Tito getting into a slightly similar piece-of-shit car.

"Hey," I yelled out to him as I fell into step behind him. "I think you dropped this." In my hand, I waved a ten-dollar bill. Not one to turn down free money, Tito came walking toward me. And I had to really force myself to hold back a grin as he took the sawbuck from my hand and turned back toward his car. When he did, I stuck the stun gun I'd been carrying into the back of Tito's neck and shot him up with a bit of pocket lightning, which, of course, dropped him to his knees. A second later, the green "charged" indicator lit up on the stun gun again and I hit Tito one more time before he could scream. Quickly, I snatched the keys from his hand, dragged his unconscious body to his car and shoved him into the trunk. From my backpack came my fake eyeglasses and a baseball cap, and I started his car and drove away.

Two blocks later, I pulled into the parking lot of a K-Mart and drove around back. There I got out and popped the trunk. Tito was slowly gaining consciousness. I wound two layers of duct tape around his mouth then bound his wrists together. I grabbed his feet and with a box cutter, I sliced his Achilles tendons. I cut them deep until I hit bone, just to make sure. I really had to hold back because having that blade in my hands, I really wanted to do him right there, carve him up like a Christmas goose. If I'd had a serrated knife, I think I would have.

I got in the car and drove.

Death Valley is nothing but desert for hundreds of miles. Out there copper mining is still big business but it isn't anything you can see from any of the major highways. Same goes for crystal meth, which I believe accounts for a lot of the dirt roads cut into the scrub off the beaten path. In the distance, I could see the lights from one of the mines still going, but best guess was it was set back at least ten miles away. Other than that, you might as well have been on the dark side of the moon.

I'd bought the tri-fold entrenching shovel at an Army Navy Surplus store last year because I knew it would eventually come in handy and it would fit nicely in my backpack. As convenient as it was, it made kind of a shitty shovel. If I ever had to dig a foxhole with one of these things, I would have lost my mind. It took me an hour to make a three-foot deep shallow grave. I was willing to dig longer but started to get afraid the battery on Tito's crappy car would run out and leave me stranded there as well. Three feet would have to do. I still had more work ahead of me. I wasn't done quite yet.

Tito was conscious when I popped open the trunk. I shined my flashlight on him and when the light caught his eyes, I could see how scared he was. My heart thundered. I got so excited, I think I broke into a grin and laughed. I don't remember for sure.

Then I grabbed his arm and pulled him out, dropping him onto the ground.

"You're free to go, Tito," I told him.

And when he tried to stand up his ankles gave out from under him. He must have had a rush of adrenaline, because he actually managed two running steps before collapsing. I let him try again, even helping him up, and when he fell again, I almost wet myself laughing. I told him how the Achilles tendons work and how, without them, he was more fucked than Lindsay Lohan passed out on an oil rig. I told him if he didn't like it, he was free to go anytime. I dragged him in front of his headlights and pulled him up to his knees.

With the box cutter, I slashed through both the duct tape and Tito's skin so that when I tore the tape off his face, it actually opened up a flap all the way to his upper lip. I let him scream. We were too far away from anything for anybody to hear. I even joined him. I leaned down and screamed into his face.

I waited until he was out of breath before telling him who I was and why he was there.

He denied it. He denied everything.

He even tried to tell me his name wasn't Tito. I had to laugh. Eddy told me that after he'd gotten out of prison, Tito Gomez had hooked up with a fake ID based on someone else's stolen Social Security number. I told him it was just a matter of weeks or days before the DNA came back, and he would be arrested again, and that I was just saving the taxpayers a whole pile of money.

I told him about Janet Twitty's motherless two year-old, making up details about everything because I knew nothing about her kid. I just wanted Tito Gomez to feel as bad as possible.

"That kid has to go to a special shrink for toddlers because he wakes up every night from nightmares about his murdered mommy," I told him. "Janet Twitty was the only parent caring for that kid."

And the fact that it didn't seem to move Tito Gomez one bit made me so angry. He kept up with the same old crap about him not being the guy. What else was he going to say?

So annoyed was I that I lost my cool for two seconds and picked up the fold-up shovel and smashed Tito across the face with it. I hit him so hard that I knocked him over. I could see in the headlight glare that his face was bleeding.

And I started thinking again about his car battery running out on me. I could have sworn I saw the lights dim just a titch.

I grabbed Tito by his greasy hair and dragged him to the hole. He tried fighting me but with his wrists tied together it was tough. I saw him try to bite through the duct tape on his hands, so I dropped him. I rolled him over onto his stomach and rammed the pointy end of the shovel into his back just below the neck until I felt it slip between two vertebrae. There was a ka-chuck as I severed his spine like I was cutting through a thick piece of celery and then his arms and legs went totally limp as if I'd just turned his body off with the flip of a switch.

He was shrieking when I grabbed him by the hair again and dragged him to the hole. I was starting to sweat like a madman.

I asked Tito what it was like to cut into someone with a serrated blade. If he could feel each pointy edge tug at the skin and sinew when he pulled the knife out, like a saw cutting through wood. He didn't hear a word I said. He just continued shrieking.

But then I realized I had completely screwed up.

I kicked his legs. He didn't even register.

I stomped on the back of his kneecap. Nothing. There was no feeling from the neck down and I couldn't believe I didn't think of this when I paralyzed him.

The only place he was going to feel anything was on his face and neck.

I went back to the car to get the lighter fluid and matches from my backpack.

When I got back to Tito, I decided to take care of a little business first. Grabbing the shovel by the handle close to the blade, I used the point to sever Tito's right hand. Though he was bleeding, his arm just lay there like a dead fish. It took over a dozen blows with the pointy end of the entrenching tool, and I had to use the box cutter to slash away the last strands of muscle holding it on. While I was doing it, I turned Tito's head so he could see me since he disappointingly couldn't feel it.

I leaned over him and asked, "For finding you and taking you off the streets, don't I deserve a hand?"

He tried to spit at me. I spit back at him. Right on his face.

And then I asked him. "Tito, give me ten good reasons why you should live and I'll drive you to the highway and leave you there where you have a chance of someone finding you, but know that you'll probably be arrested in a few days anyway."

I meant it too.

"I have a wife and kids," he sputtered, blood and spittle flying from his mouth.

"That's one," I told him. "But if I were you, I would have said 'One I have a wife' and 'Two, I have kids'. You just wasted a perfectly good reason."

"Please don't kill me," he begged.

I told him that wasn't a reason and that he had thirty seconds to come up with the next of nine more.

He couldn't give me one.

"Time's up," I told him as I sprayed the lighter fluid into his face. He whipped his head back and forth so I squirted it onto his hair. Then I took two steps back and flicked lit matches on him until one caught.

I could hear him scream for about two seconds before he stopped. His head kept snapping back and forth, side-to-side like he was grooving to some crazy soundless techno house beat. One hundred and sixty eight beats per minute of pure head-banging frenzy.

I let it burn for about thirty seconds, not too much so it would go past second degree. Once you get down below the skin and nerves into the vascular tissue, you lose feeling and

I didn't want that so I threw a shovelful of dirt onto his face to put the flames out.

Tito's mouth was still opening and closing. I couldn't see his eyes because they were under a layer of dirt but I'm guessing there's a good chance they had been fused shut. It smelled like roast pork in the air all around us.

With my boot, I rolled him into the shallow hole. Unfortunately, he landed face down, not up like I had wanted so I had to step down and turn him over. I could see his chest still moving slightly.

It took me twenty minutes or so to fill the hole back up. I threw the first shovel full of dirt onto his face to see if I could make him move his head.

I did.

I put Tito's hand in the trunk of the car. I made it back to Laughlin before the sun came up and almost thought I would have to stop for gas. How bad would that have been? I parked Tito's car a mile from where I'd left mine.

I'll let Eddy know that's where they can find it. I'm sure they'll get enough DNA off the package in the trunk to match Janet Twitty's rape kit sample.

One more shithead off the streets. I'd like to think I'm buying my way into heaven somehow with my work.

My car was just as I'd left it. I slipped back into my room and slept for four hours like a stone, showered and caught the tail end of continental breakfast. Bad coffee and a powdered donut from a box.

Someone please tell me, on what continent does this qualify as breakfast?

As soon as I finish this, I'm going to check out and make the short drive to Vegas. Tomorrow I get naked with my Jennie Bomb. It's all I can think about.

Today I finally have zero desire for a cigarette. Maybe it's the smell of Tito Gomez's burning face and hair still stuck in my nostrils.

Maybe it's just that I don't want to smoke.

FIVE

Dear Diary,

I now know what Heaven will be like. I spent two hours with my Jennie Bomb in room 1850 of the Flamingo Hotel in Las Vegas and I can't imagine a single thing better on this green Earth.

The day didn't start so well though. Jenny called me in the morning to tell me she would be a little bit late—an hour since her driver was running behind. I couldn't believe it and at first I got really pissed off, but I didn't let it show on the phone. I had just spent a long time in the shower to get myself squeaky clean; the way Jenny likes it before she puts her tongue all over every inch of my body. I thought she was blowing me off and I almost lost my cool with her, but I didn't. I was able to stay frosty for my little Jenny Bomb. I was proud of myself. But after I got off the phone, I could see that I had sweat all the way through my silk shirt. The one I had bought special just for today because I know my Jenny likes silk and silky things. I was so mad; I ripped the fucking shirt off my body without even unbuttoning it. Now I was wet and stinking, and she was going to arrive in two hours. I jumped into the shower and scrubbed over and over until I knew I was clean again.

But when the time she was supposed to show up arrived and she wasn't here, I started to feel annoyed. After another thirty minutes, I was getting angry. I was ready to go out looking for her.

Then at a little past three she showed up. There was a knock on my hotel room door and my hands actually trembled when I reached for the knob. Standing right there in a simple black dress in front of me was the most beautiful angel I had ever seen. Blond hair, soft brown eyes, 5'2", perfect 32C breasts. Her skin flawless, like something from a painting, just radiated sex.

I had been pent-up so long, waiting for her, just fantasizing about this moment, that I got hard the moment I saw her. I couldn't help it. It was out of my control. My tent was pitched and she noticed it.

That's what makes Jennie so special, not like other girls who would see my hard-on in my pants and make a face or roll their eyes in disgust. I hate that, when they make rude comments. It's not like every girl doesn't like a good fucking. They just feel like they have to act like that in order to hold onto what little power they have. Those girls are bitches. Fucking bitches.

But Jennie's not like that at all. She loves sex and makes no secret about it. She saw my stiff cock and raised an eyebrow and gave me a grin. As she entered the room, she playfully brushed her fingertips across the front of my pants. Between that and the smell of her perfume drifting up into my nostrils, I think I almost passed the fuck out.

I closed the door and locked it behind us and she turned and gave me a big hug, grinding on me through my pants before she pulled back and gave me a long, deep wet kiss.

"How have you been, sweetie?" she asked me. My heart skipped a beat as she ran her hands down the buttons on the front of my shirt. It wasn't my silk one, which bummed me out, and I was waiting for her to say something, but she didn't.

Which is what makes her so great. She never criticizes you. She never tells you how stupid or useless you are. She never tells you to stop drinking or to take out the trash. She's just there to make you feel good. Lots of girls could learn something from her.

Her hand ran up my arm and she asked me if I'd been working out. But then she saw that some of the hairs on my arm had been singed. Must have happened the other night. I told her I was making something on the stove and there was a flare-up in the pan. I hate lying to her. I really do.

After I gave her the envelope (with a little gratuity and a nice handwritten note), she slipped out of her dress, doing a little shimmy for me, a little waggle of her hips to make it slide down her legs like raindrops running down a window. Underneath, she was wearing a red lace bra and red lace panties, but she kept on her black high heels. She undressed me, first unbuttoning my shirt. With her tongue she traced a line from the nape of my neck down to my belt, and then undid that too.

I still had my shoes on and when she pulled my pants down, I had to sit on the bed to take them off. I was angry with myself for breaking the mood, but Jennie just smiled. She knelt in front of the bed and took me into her mouth.

Of all the feelings I've ever had in the world, this had to be one of the best. All of a sudden, I was overcome with numbness all across my face as she jacked my shaft and deep-throated me. This is one place she excels. With her hand, she stroked up and over the head of my cock as her mouth came off then went all the way down to the base. The whole time, I could smell her hair, like wild lilies, and she let out these small moans that escaped from her throat.

And every time I was getting close, she could tell and would slow down. My fingers dug into the bed cover and my toes curled. At one point, my entire body was shaking. I kept watching her, looking at the delicate line of her neck. Her pale skin. I tried to reach out to touch her, but I couldn't reach since I was lying back on my elbows.

Finally, she let me come and I think I actually screamed when I did. I may have even seen a white light.

When I looked down, I saw that at some point, Jennie had slipped a condom onto me. She's good like that.

After that, we both got naked and crawled into bed together. She laid on me, her breasts brushing my chest.

And we talked. Just talked.

She told me about her yoga instructor who was writing a book and about a vegan cooking class she was taking. Last year, she went to Paris for two weeks by herself. No work, just sightseeing. I told her I'd never been to Europe. She told me I had to go sometime.

After that she asked me about how I was doing. I told her work was getting difficult because companies are spending less money and buying less but I didn't want to bore her. Besides, I was getting hard again and I still had over an hour left.

This time, I watched as she rolled the clear latex condom onto my erect cock and I told her the first time would be for me, but the second time would be for her. She understood what I meant and told me she wouldn't want it any other way. I told her to talk dirty to me. She asked how slutty? I told her as much as possible.

I got on top of her and put her legs up over my shoulders and slid into her wet pussy. I rammed her hard while she yelled, "Fuck my wet cunt," over and over. And then, I rolled her over onto her belly and took her from behind. She came once. Then twice, and started begging for me to fuck her in the ass. When I told her I wanted to, she took out a small bottle of liquid KY from her purse and put some on me, then slid a lubed-up finger into her asshole.

I was only in her for a few moments, because I couldn't hold back. It was so tight and so wonderful. I came even harder than the first time.

After she went to the bathroom to clean up, she brought a warm wet washcloth for me. We spooned in the bed and I wanted to fall asleep with her in my arms, but I was afraid to waste any of my precious time with her. She told me she had always been multi-orgasmic since the age of 13. I wanted to tell her about everything. About my true work, but I held back.

With only twenty minutes left, we fucked again, but this time, as promised, it was for her and very gentle though she kept prodding me to go harder and faster. I wanted to make her come two or three more times, give her something to remember me by. Her legs shook each time like little tremors as she bit her lip.

After she left, I was still feeling high as a cloud, like I could have walked off the roof of the Flamingo and just floated down to the sidewalk. I was so relaxed that I lay down on the bed, staring at the ceiling, thinking about her and trying to relive every little detail and fell dead asleep. When I awoke, it was sometime past seven and I looked around my empty room and started to feel depressed. I buried my face in the pillow trying to smell Jennie's scent. I pushed my nose into the middle of the mattress trying to find the smell of her pussy on the sheets. Then it hit me that at that moment it was more than likely she was with some other guy, giving him the GFE. I wanted to find that guy and snap his neck like a fucking twig.

I needed to get out of the room, so I went down to the front and hopped a cab. I could feel myself getting hungry again, so I told the driver to take me to a big shopping mall.

What you have to love about any mall is the complete anonymity of it. Everywhere I looked there were hot girls and if I was careful enough about it I could stare at them without being noticed. But that's the thing. They want to be seen. You really think they whore themselves up with the makeup, the tight pants and showing all of that cleavage for nothing?

They know what they're doing.

I saw this one little hottie in the food court, leaning against the counter, sticking her ass out. Don't try to tell me that she didn't want it.

I sat there just ten feet away and took pictures with the camera on my cell phone. Just thinking about what I wanted to do to her gave me such a boner that I had to go into the men's room to take care of myself.

Later, over by the ice cream place, I saw this blonde that may have been the most beautiful girl I've ever seen in my life (tight pink t-shirt, faded tight jeans, hair pulled back into a pony tail), sitting there licking a cone, driving me crazy.

Talking to her was a real heifer in a long black skirt. I used to think that the fat friend was a sign these hot girls had compassion. Now I've grown to think it's a sign of insecurity. I took pictures of her (the hot one, not the blimp) to jerk off to later. When they finished their ice cream (did the fatty really need two scoops and sprinkles?), I followed them across the mall.

It occurred to me that if I had some kind of business card identifying me as a talent scout for a big modeling agency I probably could have talked this girl back to my room. How hard could that be? Paris lights. New York runways. I bet if she thought there was a modeling contract in it, she'd be happy to let me get her behind closed doors and do stuff to her. She'd have a big smile on her face as she wiped my cum off of it.

I almost followed them to the parking lot but I decided not to. Too many video cameras in malls.

Last year I read about a town somewhere in the Midwest where they found out that all these high school girls were turning tricks at the mall. Not ghetto skanks, upper-middle-class white girls who would approach guys and fuck them so they could make some extra money for shoes and coke and shit like that. It was all a big goof for them. They just wanted to party and make some cash instead of giving that pussy away in some sweaty backseat down behind the mini-mart.

Can you imagine that? Some tight little teen queen hottie off the cheerleading squad?

A guy could jerk himself off to death with news like that. They're all whores. All of them.

After the mall closed, I went over to Bally's and had a couple of drinks in the lounge. Listened to some crummy four-piece mangling classic rock tunes. Not one good song in the bunch. Stopped back at the Flamingo to see if there were any really drunk girls at the karaoke bar. There was one, but she was a whale. Looked around to see if she had a hot friend. No such luck. I guess she'll just have to get by on her personality.

Went back to my room and crawled into bed. Tried to smell Jennie's pussy on the sheets again. Jerked off once, and went to sleep.

Dear Diary,

Woke up after 10. Slept like a baby. Did fifty push-ups.

On the way to the bathroom, I found a folded-up note on the floor. It was a phone number. It took me a few minutes to figure out what it meant. Then, all of a sudden, it hit me like a ton of bricks.

I went downstairs and ran to a pay phone across the street and called the number. It was Eddy.

Laughlin cops found Tito Gomez's car with a trunk full of blood and his severed hand in the back seat. Eddy asked me how well I wiped down the vehicle and I told him "top to bottom." He said it looked like the cops found a partial on the inside of the trunk lid. I told Eddy that I was sure it couldn't be mine.

But truth is I'm not sure.

I thought I got everything inside and outside, but I never reopened the trunk. If it were mine, it would have been left behind when I pulled Tito out onto the ground. I don't remember it happening.

I must be careful and ready for anything.

Even death.

SIX

Dear Diary,

It has been two weeks since my last entry and only one day since my last cigarette. Yes, I started smoking again in Vegas. Yes, I'm weak. Yes, I hate myself for it.

After talking to Eddy, and hearing about that latent print, I went to a liquor store and bought a pack and chain-smoked it, then went and bought another. I'm going to quit. I just need a little more time.

I'm giving up my hobby.

The itch is gone. Tito Gomez scratched it, especially coming right on the heels of Phil Testaleone. Two that close together is just not smart. In fact, it's incredibly stupid as hell. At first, I was pissed Eddy hasn't tried to contact me since Vegas, but then I realized it was absolutely the best thing he could have done to distance himself. He's risked so much already. But it's frustrating. I haven't heard anything about the Tito Gomez case at all in the news. If the cops have a lead on that latent print, nobody's talking.

But if they had something, I'd be in cuffs right now. And I think we all know that will never happen. I won't allow it.

All I want now is to put this all behind me. Once the itch is scratched, it goes away. I can control it. It doesn't control me.

This might be my last entry. I need to put this book away before someone finds it.

Dear Diary,

Oh My God! The Interstate Slasher struck again!

Also, I have not been able to quit smoking. It's so dirty and disgusting. I am so angry with myself that I can't even begin to describe it. Every time I'd light up I feel like I want to put a razor blade down my throat, but I can't help it. For some reason, I just didn't feel like I had the strength to put it all away.

Until yesterday. When the Interstate Slasher struck again. He'd been quiet for over four years (50 months to be precise) and just like the cops, I started thinking he'd hung up his cleats once and for all. Or maybe he had died without getting caught, every serial killer's dream.

Fourteen and oh, no arrests. Batting a thousand.

But now, he's back.

This time, it was gruesome again.

This time, it was a pretty young co-ed who had vanished while driving back to school after a long weekend at home. Staties found her car with a bag of clean laundry in the back and no signs of a struggle. Four days later, a couple of queers found her naked and mutilated body in the woods behind a rest stop when they went to do whatever queers do.

The cops know it was the Interstate Slasher because he put a broken bottle up her vagina and both her eyes were taken out. The M.O. is the same as his last victim. A twenty-year-old girl with wispy blonde hair whose car had broken down along the 15 freeway. The Slasher cut her abdomen open and dumped her by the side of the road a hundred miles away after he'd raped her. She was discovered hours later with her guts spilled onto the ground around her. An autopsy showed her own organ tissue under her nails proving she lived long enough to try to scoop up her entrails with her hands before bleeding out.

I was eating a calamari steak at some new place named Turk's that Whiney-ass wanted to try (side salad with ranch, French fries, two diet Cokes). We were just outside of the bar and they had broken into the Dodger's game with the news.

You could have knocked me over with a feather because I just knew it had to be the Interstate Slasher before the newswoman even mentioned a hint of his name. I'm tuned into that kind of thing. The hairs on the back of my neck were standing upright.

Whiney-ass is so clueless that he had no idea who the Interstate Slasher even was. What a moron. How could you not?

I tried schooling him that this was the guy who had terrorized the highways west of the Rockies by abducting, raping and killing over a dozen women over the course of the last decade or more.

He didn't want to hear about it. What a pussy. No wonder his ex-wife left him. He has the spine God gave a jellyfish. He likes being a victim. He's starting to make me sick.

I went home and watched all the newscasts. Nobody was saying anything more than I'd heard in those first few seconds.

Today's Times had a better article about it.

Apparently, this particular rest stop where the body was dumped has a reputation as a notorious homosexual anonymous sex location, enough that it's earned the nickname "Cupcake Lane".

So I figured, given how busy this Cupcake Lane supposedly is, whoever dumped that body either knew the location well enough to do it without being seen or he was incredibly lucky. The third possibility is that he so brazenly picked this location because he's trying to get caught.

Maybe. But I doubt it.

I'm pretty sure it's not that he's careless because the Interstate Slasher is meticulous in how well he cleans up any evidence when he dumps his victims. Not a single hair or fingerprint.

I am going to e-mail one of Eddy's floater accounts today to see if he'll get back to me. I'm thinking now that he owes me one. I need to see this file. I need to find out what else he knows about the Tito Gomez investigation.

Dear God, I will quit smoking forever if you please let me find the Interstate Slasher. I want this guy badly. If I could get him, I would retire.

Dear Diary,

It has been five days without a cigarette. I woke up late today.

Dreamed last night. Bad one. Arthur Tancredo and his brother Sam. We were kids again. I was running down Turkey Hill, through the woods by the creek looking for Billy and I couldn't find him. Then I see them, Arthur and Sam, holding Billy's legs.

I can't remember if I've had this one before or not.

I woke up. Stretched for only ten minutes. No time for breakfast. Put on a gray shirt, short sleeve, dark blue slacks, black socks, and black loafers I bought two years ago at Macy's from a salesman with a harelip.

No proper breakfast. Ate a granola bar on the way in. Cinnamon and raisin. 90 Calories. 1.5 grams of fat. Listened to News. Teacher's strike, now in its second week. Nothing on Interstate Slasher. Still no word back from Eddy.

Got to my desk. Sat and stared at an open Word doc for two hours. Miss Big Nose came by to get me to sign a maternity card for someone in accounting whose name I didn't recognize. She saw I'd typed only one word on the page: bleed.

I lied to her and told her I was making a list of notes a client had given me about the color separation on the PDX-2000. She didn't even care.

When she left, I added another word: more.

Then I deleted the document, and told everyone I was going on some sales calls.

Instead, I went back to Borders.

John Martin Scripps was born outside of London in 1959. He had a happy childhood until the age of 9 when he came home to find his father had put his head in the oven and offed himself. Shortly afterwards, his mother was diagnosed with throat cancer. The FBI claims 70 percent of all serial murderers have experienced a traumatic childhood event.

In 1991, he was imprisoned on the Isle of Wight for heroin smuggling. It was during this time in the joint that the powers-that-be decided a valuable part of his rehabilitation would be learning a trade so Scripps was trained to be a butcher's assistant.

Specifically, he was instructed how to use a knife to cut up a carcass.

While on a four-day leave in 1994, Scripps fled the country. After a few weeks, he ended up in Mexico where he befriended a British backpacker named Timothy McDowell whom Scripps beat to death, then dismembered, before tossing his Limey ass (and the rest of him) into an alligator-infested river.

In March of 1995, Scripps, now in Singapore, ran into a British traveler names Gerard Lowe who was having trouble finding lodging. Kindly enough, Scripps offered to share his. Within moments of entering Room 1511 of the River View Hotel, Scripps smashed Lowe on the head from behind with a three-pound camping hammer. Before Lowe died, he gave up his bankcard pin to Scripps, who then put his butchering skills to use. In an interview much later, Scripps described the dismemberment in great detail, especially how he cut through Lowe's throat and then twisted the knife through the back of the neck to take off Lowe's head.

"Just like a pig," said Scripps.

He cut off Lowe's arms at the elbows and then took off the upper arms at the shoulders by slipping the boning knife through the ball and socket joints. No sawing was necessary.

With the legs, he stuck the knife into the hip joint, twisting and cutting until they came loose. The knees he cut until they snapped back, so they could be folded up, along with the rest of Lowe, into a suitcase. The whole process took several hours of meticulous work. Later that night

Scripps took a taxi to Singapore Harbor where he dumped Lowe into the water off Clifford Pier.

Later, I went into the men's room at Borders and after finishing my business, I was washing my hands and found a single dark hair on the sink top. Just one. I started thinking it might come in handy at some point so I folded it up inside a paper towel and stuck it in my pocket.

Listened to the radio on the way home. Double shot Tuesday. Joan Jett and the Blackhearts singing "Bad Reputation" and "I Love Rock and Roll". Turned it up so loud my ears started ringing. Stopped and picked up a whole rotisserie chicken and a side of rice pilaf. Same blonde behind the counter (acne is getting worse). With some makeup, she would look a bit like my Jennie Bomb. She would look good. When she gave me my change, her fingers brushed my hand. I'm not sure if it was on purpose.

Definitely a new logo on their bag. Bolder colors.

I've read where artists often hide pagan symbols in their commercial work. Nothing you would ever notice, but your subconscious does. Often times it's with the consent of the client who will use the fact that all humans have a death wish to their marketing advantage.

This new symbol on the bag. I think there's something hidden in there. I can't stop looking at it.

And I do think she brushed her fingers against my hand on purpose. How could it not have been? What is she? C cup? Nice on her frame. I wonder if I tell her I'm a talent scout if she'd believe me. I might get in the car and go back there later to see if she's still working. I wonder if she drives or takes the bus?

I could find out if I wanted.

For some reason she reminds me of that girl from the Duran Duran song.

Her name is Rio and she dances on the sand...

Sheila Damude, a 50 year-old Canadian woman was traveling on vacation to Bangkok, Thailand with her son. At Phuket airport, they met John Martin Scripps at the baggage carousel waiting for his luggage. They asked if he knew of any good hotels. He directed them to Nilly's Marina Inn, where a beachside room would cost them $18 a night. The very same hotel where he was staying.

Before noon the next day, Scripps entered their room and, after beating them to death with his hammer, dismembered their bodies as he had with Gerald Lowe. He then took their passports, credit cards and money and went on a bit of a shopping spree. The severed limbs, skulls and torsos of the Damudes were found over the course of a couple of weeks, scattered around the countryside.

After being sentenced to hang, Scripps was confined to an eight-foot-by-six-foot jail cell. His last meal was pizza and a cup of hot cocoa. He then wrote a short final note, which in part read:

Can I be a person again? Only time will tell me. What really upset me was when you are told every day that you are not a member of the human race.

When the guards came for Scripps at 3:30 am on the day of his hanging, he fought them tooth and nail. It took 12 guards 20 minutes to drag him to the gallows, during which time he suffered a broken nose, jaw and cheekbone, plus two black eyes.

Nothing has ever been written of what damage he was able to inflict on them, fighting his last fight.

He had refused to put on civilian clothes so he was taken to the gallows naked. Scripps had also purposely not let his captors put him on a scale beforehand. They miscalculated in judging his weight and as a result used too long a rope. When the trap door opened under Scripps' feet, his head was nearly torn off from the excessive fall.

Dear Diary,

Rio was picked up five minutes after work by an older man driving a Volvo (V50 station wagon, white, license plate 856HAX). Must be her dad, though that's just a guess. I'm not sure if fathers know that every straight man wonders to himself what it would be like to fuck his daughter?

SEVEN

Dear Diary,

Woke up today a half hour before the alarm. I hate that. Did 100 sit-ups. Stretched and all of my joints popped like gunshots. I need to get in better shape if there's any chance of getting the Interstate Slasher. Still no news.

Seven days without a cigarette. If I can make it to tomorrow morning, a whole week off, it'll be easy. Seven days without a smoke makes one week. One week. One week. I can do it.

This morning: Eggbeaters omelet with ham and cheese and a plain bagel with butter. Someone threw a bottle from a moving car at one of the groups of picketing teachers. Nobody got a license plate. Apparently not everybody is supportive of their demands for higher wages.

Just goes to show you what kind of world we live in. There is a plague of ignorance and complacency afflicting the human race. God forbid we are inconvenienced or put out by the needs of others. We are the soft and weak. Undisciplined zombies addicted to our microwave popcorn, no-fault divorce, get-rich-quick lifestyle. We have entitlement issues and a lousy work ethic, which, let me tell you, is not life's perfecta. We are bitter. We are bodies in motion that stay in motion. We keep up with the Joneses. We read gossip columns and tabloids. We watch TMZ, Access Hollywood, Extra, and Entertainment Tonight and then complain when someone violates our privacy. We have the attention span of gnats. We preach tolerance from inside the protection of cloistered groups. We will happily give up our rights in the name of liberty.

Until the day we die.

And then, at that point, what the fuck does it matter? Death is the only pure state of being.

In the obits today:

Thomas J. Bonney, passed away on August 6 at his home in Santa Monica, California.

Born in Huntsville, Texas on December 3, 1915, he left school to support his family as a performer in a traveling carnival. In 1933, he moved to California and later became an apprentice in the makeup department at MGM Pictures, eventually getting promoted to Head Artist in 1965, a position he held for the next 21 years.

Thomas worked on hundreds of motion pictures including: "Singin' in the Rain", "North by Northwest", "Logan's Run" and "Young Frankenstein".

He is survived by his wife of 41 years, Cecilia Bonney, his son Jack and daughter Gwendolyn.

Do you think Thomas J. Bonney cares right now whether or not the neighbor's dog craps on his lawn? Do you think he gives a flying fuck at a rolling donut about whether his clothes are being washed in "New and Improved" Tide with Bleach? I need to feel something. I'm going to Thomas J. Bonney's funeral. I need to touch his casket.

Spent two hours at my desk, phoning customers to see what else they needed. In between fractured bouts of pretending like I gave a shit about my client's problems I phoned the chicken place. When a guy answered, some managerial-sounding ultra-douche I hung up, but later when a girl picked up, with her light and wafer-thin voice, I held on the line as she kept asking "Hello? Hello?" as I tried to tune my ear to hear her breathe. After a few awkward moments, I realized I had been fondling myself and I could feel the pre-cum sticking the head of my cock to the inside of my shorts.

I went to the break room to get a root beer but saw they had changed from Barq's to A&W so I got a Diet Coke, and then started to regret the impulse as I pressed the button. Instead, I put another buck into the machine and got the A&W. As I turned, there was Miss Big Nose standing there going through her purse.

"Here," I said, handing her the Diet Coke. Just as I was at the door, she turned to me and said, "Are you trying to say something?" while holding up the can.

I wanted to tell her I'd bought it by accident and she was welcome to it, but it somehow all came out wrong. Instead of trying again, I turned and walked out. Sheesh, try to be nice to someone and they shit all over you.

Everyone around the office is nervous because apparently The Fossil is coming down from the head office in Scottsdale. The guy's run the company for fifty years with the idea that nobody should ever feel like they have job security—the management credo of the modern age—the culture of fear.

Word is The Fossil will be cutting some heads when he gets here. That I'd actually like to see. Literally, I mean. Hell, I'd even help the old man. I'd hold down some of the management team and sharpen the machete.

I can just see my boss' face the moment that blade came down on his scalp. I can hear the hissing sound a skull makes when split open.

Stopped at an auto parts store on the way home because I saw on the Internet how you could make a working silencer from a slightly customized oil filter. Nobody suspects a guy with an oil filter in the trunk of his car.

I started to think a lot about that dream. Arthur Tancredo and his brother Sam. I can now still see their faces. I hadn't thought of them in years. But that dream. Did it really happen that way? I know how it ended because I can still hear their screams and smell the burning of their flesh. Christ, we were all just kids. It's funny how something so important at one point can just slip your mind like yesterday's grocery list.

If I close my eyes, I can see what they were wearing. Arthur's red plaid shirt and overalls and Sam in that T-shirt for that Saturday morning kid's cartoon. What was that? It's on the tip of my tongue. If I close my eyes, I can hear the click of the lock being snapped shut in the hasp, the strike of matches against the back cover of the matchbook. Some memories don't stay buried forever, I suppose.

Dear Diary,

Eddy finally wrote back. No apologies for going AWOL on me, no information about the Tito Gomez case. Just an e-mail with a note saying: "Thought you might find this interesting" and a single address in Mission Viejo.

No indication why I'd find it interesting. Guess that means I'm getting in the car tonight. Thanks a lot, Eddy.

Mission V? You gotta be fucking kidding me. I generally try to avoid Orange County as much as possible. There's a level of phoniness you get used to in L.A. but once you get behind the Orange Curtain, my asshole meter is constantly getting pinned. Especially anytime some surfer or silicone housewife opens their unenlightened cakehole. I'm not necessarily in the mood to make the drive down there but it's obvious Eddy wants me to see something.

Is he toying with me?

Holy shit... is this the Interstate Slasher? Could it be that Eddy has tracked him down like I asked?

How would I know if it is him? Nobody's ever seen his car. Or at least, I mean nobody who has lived. If I only had some of that stuff cops spray to identify bloodstains. Where would they sell that?

I know what it's called.

Luminol.

I'm taking my kit. I'm leaving right now.

Dear Diary,

Sat in traffic all the fucking way down there. Stopped near Anaheim to get a burger (double with cheese, seasoned fries, large Coke) and to pee. No cute girls behind the counter. Was so busy looking at the menu trying to decide what poison I wanted that I didn't even realize I had gotten into the line with the retarded kid with Down Syndrome or Mongoloidism or whatever you call it and it took him far too long to order six packages of cookies. What the fuck did he need six packs of shitty, dry cookies for anyway?

I drove to the address that Eddy sent me. 404 Winter Lane. There was a fairly late model Caddy in the driveway. I drove past once and saw there was a light on in one of the bedrooms on the second floor. Looked like a single lamp— possibly bedside combined with the shimmer of a TV screen. I checked my watch and at half past 11, both the light and the TV went out. Right after the late news perhaps. Working man? Nine to fiver? How do I even know it was a man?

I snuck up to the house and tried peeking into the windows. No dice. Shades drawn all the way to the bottom. I didn't try to open them. Double-paned with alarm company stickers on them.

Neighbor's dog started barking, so I left quietly and napped in the car behind a strip mall. I went back to Winter Lane a couple of hours later and the whole street was quiet as church. I watched the house for a while. Nothing. The neighbor's dog must have gone back inside, because the barking had stopped. I've read how burglars will often bring hot dogs soaked in poison in order to silence a dog. I'd never hurt an animal unless my life depended on it.

Mailbox was empty.

I checked the Caddy. Deville, white, good condition, no idea how old—maybe five years, at most. License plate 5ZU-B88. I felt around under the chassis, in the wheel well and the bumper for one of those magnetic hide-a-key boxes. No luck. After a while, I had to give up before someone saw me. I got in my car and drove all the way home sure that Eddy had sent me on a wild goose chase.

I blasted the radio all the way back up the 5 until I hit town. I was feeling edgy, annoyed. I really wanted a cigarette.

It was late, but I headed downtown. I had to let off some steam

Down past the Staples Center, I found a couple of streetwalkers. One in a short denim jacket and jeans. The other in what looked like a discarded bridesmaid's dress. Both were rail thin. Probably crack whores.

I kept driving until I got to 4th Street. There I saw a chubby redhead in a short green dress. The way she eyed my car, I could tell she was a working girl. I drove around the block looking for cop cars or vans or anybody sitting around in a sedan. I'd hate to have to ask Eddy for help on that one.

Still I wasn't about to throw caution to the wind. At the light, I opened my kit and took out a long, thin flathead screwdriver and stuck it in the pouch behind the passenger seat.

When I pulled up, Red was all smiles. I told her I was just looking for a little head. She checked me up and down, checked the car, and asked if I was a cop. I told her I wasn't, but I play one on the Internet. She laughed. I don't know if she really thought it was funny or if I was just a good salesman. When she leaned in closer, I could see the scar on her cheek and the bags under her eyes. Her mouth looked right. It wasn't like I was searching for a date for the prom.

I took fifty bucks out of my pocket and gave it to her as she got into the passenger seat. She told me there was an alley nearby. Not so fast, I thought. I pull into some alley and her pimp knocks me over the head and rolls me. I lied that I had a childhood fear of alleys. She just shrugged. I pulled down a side street behind a construction site I had passed a couple blocks away.

"I'll give you another ten bucks," I told her because I could see she was agitated we were spending more time in the car than she wanted to. I put it in park with the engine running and eased my seat back as I pulled out my cock. She made me put a condom on. Her face dropped onto me instantly.

Her mouth felt good on me, even with the rubber. Santana's "Oye Como Va" was playing on the radio. I took a moment to look around to make sure we were alone here. I started thinking about the house on Winter Lane in Mission V. then pushed it out of my mind. Red started jacking me hard. She meant business.

I could smell her cheap perfume mixed with a bit of B.O. I could see the roots in her hair in the dim light coming through the windshield with the slight gray at the scalp. Thinking about how pathetic she was got me more aroused. I could feel myself ready to come as I stared at the soft skin on the back of her neck.

Her head bobbed up and down on me faster.

With my right hand, I quietly reached for the thin screwdriver.

She began jacking my shaft harder. I could feel my dick ready to explode.

And it happened so fast. I nutted into her mouth and the moment she pulled off of me, I stuck the thin flat blade of the screwdriver into the base of her skull and shoved it hard upwards into her brain.

Her whole body stiffed like I'd run a 220-volt line through her muscles and I twisted the screwdriver as I held her hair and I knew the moment I pulled that blade out she'd start spraying blood so I carefully yanked up the back of her dress and used it to apply pressure to the wound.

And then she moved. I thought I had killed her, but her legs began to spasm. I got freaked out because I knew I had pulled my dick out of her mouth just moments before her jaw clamped shut. All of a sudden I was overcome by the powerful stench of shit as her bowels emptied and I could see the dark spot on the back of her dress widen across her ass. I didn't know what to do. Honestly, I panicked and hit the gas, but the car wasn't in gear. I pushed her away from me into the passenger seat and put my car in drive and pulled away from there as fast as I could. It was past 2 a.m. and I was pretty far away from my place. I knew I had to get off the surface streets before the cops came. I rolled down the windows to get the stink of her shit out of my nostrils. I ran a light and got up on the freeway and I looked over. She was slumped in her seat and I could hear her moaning so I turned up the radio, which was still playing "Oye Como Va".

I wanted to just open her door and dump her on the freeway, but I knew someone would see me.

I didn't know what to do so I drove her to another construction site I had seen up in the Valley while killing time after a dead-end sales call. And it struck me that I probably could have dumped her by the one we were at when I stabbed her, but I had freaked. By the time I got up there, it was past 3 and I was exhausted, running only on adrenaline, but I knew I couldn't get sloppy. I made it up past Northridge to Porter Ranch. Yuppieville, U.S.A. There wasn't a single house light on anywhere. I slowed down but it was too quiet.

Besides, she was still alive. I could hear her breathing slightly even though the radio was cranked. Coming from her throat was a death rattle and I closed the windows as to not make too much noise, but now I was trapped inside with the stink. I turned down another street near the canyon, and I saw the overpass to the 118 freeway. I stopped the car underneath. Next to me was a steep embankment going down to a culvert. I couldn't breathe in there. I knew I had to act quickly before anybody else drove by.

But before I did anything, I had an idea. I reached into my knapsack and took out the folded up paper towel. Inside was the single dark hair I had found on the sink in the men's room at Borders. I pulled open her collar and put it inside her dress and then opened the door and pushed her out and watched as her body tumbled down into the culvert before driving away.

EIGHT

Dear Diary,

Called in sick to work for the second day in a row. It's not a complete lie, since I really was feeling like hell yesterday. When the alarm went off, I started shaking. I had gotten no more than an hour and a half of shuteye, but it was bad sleep, the kind of bothered slumber that feels like cold and wet November rain I thought a couple cups of coffee could fix it, make me whole again but when I stumbled to the bathroom and remembered what I had done with Red, I threw up on myself.

Honestly, I don't really know what happened to me. I swear that is not who I am. A monster I am not. I was tired and something inside me snapped momentarily. It happens to everyone. I was so shaky I couldn't get off the floor. A cheap street whore probably deserved so much better (though what did she have anyway aside from abuse and struggle?) I called in to the office and talked to one of the young girls in H.R. (the annoying one, not the semi decent-looking one) and told them I had come down with a bad case of food poisoning. I crawled back into bed, but it was trash day and the truck rumbled by and woke me up an hour later from a dead sleep

I wanted to close my eyes again, but I kept thinking about how that whore kept moaning in the passenger seat as I was speeding up the freeway to the Valley. I had the music loud. I had the windows down, but still I could hear her mumble every couple of minutes. I don't know who "Sadie" is, but I'm hoping like hell it was her cat.

Nothing I can do about it now.

I remembered my car and went down. In the light of day, there was a lot more blood visible on the seat than I thought there would be. Luckily my spot in the carport is between the wall and the Toyota belonging to the old woman who never drives anymore. When I opened the door, I gagged and threw up again in the dumpster. The smell was unbelievable.

At first I thought I could maybe just spray a whole can of Lysol in there before I got inside, but realized how suspicious that might look if any of the old people who live here happen to be looking out their windows waiting for a pension check or some QVC stuff to arrive. That's the kind of behavior people remember. A broken pattern is as evident as a black eye.

A little mentholatum rub under my nose was enough to get me inside the door though I thought I was going to pass out.

There's a coin-operated car wash a mile away from me. I couldn't risk it. I drove ten miles to one I thought would be deserted. No such luck. I pulled the car into the stall, plugged four bucks in quarters into the machine and pretended to wash my car. When nobody was looking, I opened the door and pointed the spray nozzle on the passenger side. Even standing outside the car I could smell her waste seeping into my nostrils. I can only hope nobody else caught a whiff of it when they were stopped at a light next to me.

The passenger seat and carpet were soaked by the time I was done. I hit them up with the soap, but I accidentally turned the dial to hot wax because I was so tired. When I went to change it, my time ran out.

I pulled up to the large coin-op wet/dry vacs and it took me ten minutes to soak up all the water inside the car along with all the sludgy pieces of her waste. The car looked a hundred times better, but when I got in and sat on my wet driver's seat, I could still smell it. It still stunk, but now it stunk of shit and hot wax.

So with the water soaking through my pants, I drove another five miles to a different coin-op car wash and I repeated the whole thing (this time without the wax). A young kid getting quarters to wash his beater Camaro saw me spraying the nozzle inside the open door.

"Dude, you're getting your inside car wet."

I told him my kid threw up. He didn't care. What kind of fucking education are these kids receiving? *Getting my inside car wet?* Would anybody miss an idiot like that? I highly doubt it.

Again it took me another ten minutes to sop up my inside car and I could see from the water dripping from behind the glove box lid that I had managed to soak everything in there as well.

And the car still smelled bad. So I drove back to the car wash near me and did the whole thing a third time. My hands were so pruned and my fingers were getting stiff. I ended up getting soaked when I momentarily lost my grip on the spray nozzle.

I noticed the vending machine that sold cheap drying cloths (giant paper towel sheets for fifty cents each) also had those pine tree air fresheners. I bought two.

I'm also smoking again. I hate myself. I couldn't help it. I didn't want to, but after I got home I changed and opened a beer. All I could think about was how good a cigarette would taste right then. It beat thinking about all the other stuff, so I went out and bought a pack. This is it. Last pack. When I'm done, I'm done.

Dear Diary,

Today was Thomas J. Bonney's funeral. I arrived at the church late enough to not be forced into having contact with the family, but early enough to pick a good seat—one a short distance from a fire door, just in case I had to make a quick exit. You never know.

I remember the exact way I felt, my heart racing, the tears burning in my eyes, the moment I saw Billy lying there on the ground. His small body was twisted almost the whole way around and his legs were splayed at sickening angles. One had been broken so badly that the bone stuck straight through the fur just above his back right paw.

I picked him up in my arms and he nearly folded in half. I knew right away they had broken his back.

He had only been a puppy. I had barely even had him a year. Billy had been a present to me from my dad the previous fall right after he found out he had lung cancer, the inoperable kind. He told me it was so I could have someone to take along fishing or play catch with since he wouldn't be able to. He told me it was so I'd always have a friend by my side. And when he gave me the puppy, it felt so warm and small in my hands. I named it after him since his name was Will. My dad died two months later.

We had to move from our house to an apartment in another town. I never liked it there. My mother wasn't around much since she had to take a second job. I spent a lot of time outdoors, especially down by the lake since it was quiet there. I didn't make a lot of friends. Nobody ever likes the new kid.

As I stood there, cradling Billy in my arms, bawling my eyes out, Sam Tancredo came up to me and stuck his face in mine. "Well that's one less dog making noise in the neighborhood." Arthur laughed at me and called me a crybaby. "All bad dogs go to Hell," he snickered before they turned and walked away.

Later that day, after I buried Billy under a tree behind our apartment building, I went to the Tancredo's house. In my hands, I was carrying the gas can our building manager used to fill up the lawn mower and a book of matches I had taken from the kitchen counter right next to my mom's menthol Kool's.

At first I was going to burn the Tancredo's house down. But as I walked up their driveway, I had this bizarre feeling I was going to fail, that I'd be caught in the act and be sent to the nuthatch where they put fucked-up kids. Plus, I started to think there was actually no way I'd be able to burn their entire four bedroom house to the ground.

And then I saw Sam's bike just laying there a few feet away right where I figured he had dropped it before heading inside for dinner. Right away I knew what I was going to do. There was no hesitation. I picked up Sam's bike and rode it away.

I don't know how long ago they shut down the old rail yard, but I used to go there sometimes and look at the abandoned train cars and imagine I could get on one of them and go far away from there. Every now and then, I'd see an old hobo but most of them barely opened their booze-addled eyes to me. Those who did seemed to shrink away into the shadows like pale, strung-out ghosts. Even the teenagers avoided this place because some kid got knifed there once. If my mother knew that's where I was, she would have tanned my hide until I couldn't walk.

The next day after school, I found Arthur Tancredo at his locker. He was a year older than me, but still seemed much less brave without his evil shit brother or their friends around. I told him where he could find Sam's bike and walked away down the crowded hallway. Actually, I ran because I didn't want him to catch me.

Also because I wanted to beat them to the yard.

They showed up twenty minutes after me, riding tandem on Arthur's bike. The old wooden equipment shed had long been emptied and when I went inside, it smelled very lived in. Inside there was an old blanket that I kicked out of the way as I chained Sam's bike to an exposed wall beam.

"Help me with this." I could hear Sam calling out to his brother. At first I thought Arthur wouldn't go in, but he did, no doubt thinking of the pounding they were going to lay on me when they found me.

I slipped out from behind my hiding space holding the second of the brand new locks I had bought that morning (the other one was on the bike chain inside) and within the blink of an eye shut the only door to the shed and snapped the lock onto it.

I let them bang on the inside of the door in the dark and curse me. "I'm gonna fucking kill you!" Sam shouted.

I told them my dad got me that dog and that he was dead now.

"You're going to join him in a second!" Sam shouted.

"Let us out of here!" screamed Arthur and I could hear the fear in his voice. I liked that. As I poured the contents of the gas can on the walls and door I imagined what Billy must have felt when they were kicking him and holding him underwater, wondering why I wasn't there to save him.

When I struck the match, I thought I could hear Arthur sobbing. Maybe it was my imagination hoping I was hearing him sobbing.

It didn't take long for Arthur and Sam Tancredo to start screaming, their heavy breaths pulling thick smoke into their lungs.

It didn't take them long to stop either.

The dry wood caught fast. The small shed burned to the ground in less than twenty minutes. I thought for sure the smoke would bring a fire truck or a police car. Later I realized there were probably so many hobo fires here, the authorities just stopped showing up.

More than 100 people came for Thomas J. Bonney's funeral. As you entered the chapel, there was a pile of photocopies of some of the hymns. I've heard this one before:

> *I know that my Redeemer lives;*
> *O the sweet joy this sentence gives!*
> *He lives, he lives, who once was dead;*
> *he lives, my ever living Head.*

The rest of it doesn't do as much for me as this first part.

Catholic funeral. Stand up. Sit Down. Stand Up. Sit Down. Stand. Sit.

It's like funeral aerobics.

There were a number of older folks there, probably Thomas J. Bonney's colleagues in the movie industry. I'm guessing that because I've never seen so much plastic surgery. One woman sitting near me had her face pulled back so tight it looked like she couldn't close her mouth all the way. Her skin was stretched so thin I wondered if she'd rip her face in half if she sneezed.

The priest came by with the incense pot, which smelled like a moldy cigar. He wore a purple robe that looked like velvet and a lace shawl that looked like a giant doily.

Stand up. Sit Down.

After some debate, I decided to go to the internment. Thomas J. Bonney's widow cried, as did his family and most of his friends as they lowered his casket into the ground. I got the feeling he was pretty well liked.

You still have to wonder what secrets he left behind. A stash of fetish porn? An illegitimate child overseas? A gay lover in Toluca Lake? Maybe we'll never know. Everybody leaves behind secrets.

I stuck around after it was over and wandered among the graves and smoked a cigarette. A woman surprised me when she came up behind me and asked to bum a smoke. This was my last pack so I was hesitant for a second, but decided not giving her one would be suspicious. She took it and I lit it for her.

She asked how I knew Tom. I told her my dad used to work with Tom at the studio and that I met him a few times as a boy. She just nodded and changed topics. We chatted about the weather for a couple of minutes. It seemed like she just needed someone to talk to. She was cute but I figured the more I talked, the better chance I have of blowing my cover, so I finished my cigarette.

"Funny how you never really miss someone until they're dead," she said.

I nodded my head, told her it was nice meeting her and then I left.

On the way home, I stopped at the chicken place. My little blonde wasn't there again so I left. Decided to order a pizza instead.

Velvet Mouse. That was the name of the cartoon character on Sam's T-shirt. I used to watch that show when I was a kid. I don't think they air it anymore.

When I got home, I Googled the local pizza place to get a phone number and it hit me all of a sudden what I should have done in the first place. I typed in 404 Winter Lane, Mission Viejo.

Nothing.

I e-mailed Eddy. I told him I went all the way down to Mission V. I told him I didn't understand what I was looking for. I asked point blank if he was fucking with me. I hit send. I was actually fuming.

Unbelievably, ten minutes later he e-mailed back. His note asked if I was the one fucking with him. If I was really taking all of this as seriously as I should. It was unclear if he was pissed or not. You can never judge tone in an e-mail unless they use smiley faces and Eddy's not an emoticon type of guy.

I opened the attachment. I couldn't believe what he sent. It was a scan of a newspaper article.

Bronwyn Baker, age 40, acquitted of drowning her three children in the bathtub, ages 7, 4 and 18 months. Her address was right in the story. Had I done real research instead of just relying on Google, I would have found it on my own.

I think I need to read this some more and make another trip down there.

NINE

Dear Diary,

Henry Lee Lucas' father was a habitual drunken hobo who fell off a freight train and had both his legs severed by its grinding and unforgiving steel wheels. His mother was a prostitute with two teeth and a nasty habit of violence. Growing up, the Lucases were so poor most of the food they ate was either stolen or scrounged from trashcans. On the first day of school, Henry Lee had no clothes and was forced by his mother to wear a dirty dress. One teacher took pity on him and brought him real clothes. Her name, no lie, was Annie Hall.

A Woody Allen movie, Henry Lee's life was not.

At the age of 13, Henry Lee saw a girl four years his senior standing alone at a bus stop. He cornered her on an embankment and then attempted to rape her before strangling her to death. It was at this same age that Henry Lee claimed he was forced into bestiality by a half brother that made him slit the throats of animals and then have sex with them.

Isn't family wonderful?

Bronwyn Baker, 404 Winter Lane, Mission Viejo, CA.

I want to go down there and pay her a visit but I need to be careful. Her trial ended four months ago. I can't imagine her neighbors still want her living on their street. There have to be eyes on her place whether it's the guy next door or a cop rolling by to make sure nobody torches the joint.

Acquitted.

I read the story. She was the only one at home. She claimed someone broke in while she was sleeping and drowned her kids.

Someone ran the bathtub and drowned three kids and she didn't hear? C'mon.

She testified she was a heavy sleeper. Has been all her life. C'mon.

The D.A. in Orange County couldn't try his way out of a sandwich bag. Maybe if he'd been working on his case instead of his tan, they would have convicted Bronwyn Baker. It makes me very angry. Our justice system stinks.

I need to find a way inside that house. Sure I could force my way in, but I need an easy way out. I'm going down there to scout it out. Maybe tonight.

Dear Diary,

Strange thing happened at work today. Sometime soon The Fossil is supposed to show up. Head-cutting week and the sheep are nervous. I think Whiney-ass thinks he's going to get fired.

He asked me twice if I've heard anything. Two times in twenty minutes. The second time I threatened him with my stapler. I was only half-joking.

Honestly, I could care less if they let me go. I've been here long enough that my severance package could carry me for a while, and then I could collect unemployment while I focus on my real job. Maybe it would give me the kick in the ass to find a way to do this professionally. I should really talk to Eddy. I wonder if he's grooming me for something.

But with more time to research and track down information, I could do more good than I can right now with this shitty McJob as my albatross. I could focus all my energy on what I was meant to do.

There's a difference between a job and a calling. A calling consumes you. It becomes your passion every waking moment of your life. Most people drift aimlessly through life searching for a calling and never find it. But then again, most people drown in their own delusions and have very unrealistic expectations.

Just watch American Idol.

I'm lucky. I found my calling. Or maybe it found me. Either way, every day I feel alive.

Except for when I'm here in this office.

I pretended I was busy, but spent an hour surfing TheEroticReview.com for independent providers here in town. If I could only find a local version of my Jennie Bomb, I'd be a happy man, but there's only one Jennie Bomb.

One guy mentioned getting a "kinda, sorta GFE" with a girl named Luscious. I'm not looking for "kinda, sorta". This is L.A., the Girlfriend Experience probably means I have to buy her some tits and get her a part on a TV show or something.

So then I go outside to smoke one of my last cigarettes in peace and quiet and whom do I find out there, but Miss Big Nose (white blouse, grey striped skirt slightly above the knee, black shoes, slight heel).

She said she didn't know that I smoked.

I told her I had lots of secrets.

Note to self: saying something like this to a single divorcee in her late thirties is much like throwing chum into shark-infested waters. She gave me that raised eyebrow that told me much more than I needed to know about my prospects.

After a minute of blissful silence, she thanked me for giving her the Diet Coke the other day. She said she was kidding around when she asked if giving her a diet soda meant I was implying anything.

"You didn't have to run out of there," she said with a smile.

"Yes I did," I stated. I was about to tell her I felt like I was about to again.

"Oh honey, don't tell me single older women frighten you."

"I think they frighten everybody," I replied. She waited for me to finish my cigarette and we went back into the building together. At the elevator she mentioned that she and some friends were going for drinks after work at some bar I'd never heard of.

"It's a dive," she said. I told her I'd think about it.

Whiney-Ass came over to my desk to tell me that The Fossil was coming in tomorrow for sure. He was told by one of the girls in accounting that nobody's safe and management is nervous. I told him if management were doing its job instead of making people fill out reports nobody gives a shit about they would have nothing to be nervous about.

Just to fuck with him I lied and said I thought I heard someone mention his name. He went pale as a sheet. I told him I was kidding, and he stalked away angry. Good for him, showing an actual emotion other than complaining.

Complaining isn't an emotion, is it? Should be.

All this bullshit at the office was starting to stress me out, so I snuck out early. I went to a Starbucks and tried to think of what I was going to do about 404 Winter Lane. I could follow Bronwyn Baker out of the house, but that would involve staking out her place and that might be suspicious. Besides, who knows what kind of reporters or cops are on her tail.

Besides, I had to see the scene of the crime before I passed judgment.

I was just going to have to go down there and check out the house again. Look for a way in. Sometimes luck is on your side.

Then again, you never can tell what kind of luck it is until it's too late.

The pasty-faced Starsucks manager was giving me the stink eye, so I packed up and left. I checked my watch and I don't know what came over me, but I went over to that dive bar Miss Big Nose told me about.

And when I showed up, the only person from the office there was I. I felt like such a douche. I turned to walk out just as she came in through the front door, all by herself.

"You all alone?" she asked.

I told her The Fossil was in the back grilling up some sandwiches.

I was about to take off, make some excuse. I wanted to go by the chicken place to look for the blonde. Big Nose talked me into staying for a drink. I didn't answer for a moment. Just stood there because I knew she was going to say it.

"My treat."

Bingo. Single older women are so predictable.

I was feeling pretty stressed so a drink wasn't a bad idea. Might clear my head before I drive down to Mission V.

Big Nose started telling me she knew nothing about me —only that I slip in and out of the office like a ghost and never socialize with anyone.

I told her I like to keep to myself.

"Better be careful," she said. "People are going to start thinking you're the Interstate Slasher."

I nearly froze. I couldn't believe she said that. It must have shown because she got very apologetic, telling me she didn't mean to offend me and that she was only joking.

I played her like a cheap concertina. I told her the Interstate Slasher murdered my sister. She was horrified. I made up some details about how he'd cut her ears off (which is what he did with his second victim). Big Nose sat there with her hand up to her open mouth.

"Gotcha!" I exclaimed. She didn't think it was funny at first, and then laughed. And then ordered another drink. I stuck around for a second gin and tonic, and then a third.

Later, because of the booze, we ended up in the front seat of Big Nose's car making out in the parking lot of the bar.

And at some point with her hot breath on my neck and my hand inside her blouse I noticed the traffic light at the corner flashing red.

And it hit me.

"I live pretty close to here," she said with her hand on my crotch.

"I'm not that kind of guy," I told her. I was kidding, but she took it wrong.

"What are you trying to say? That I'm some kind of slut?"

You know that feeling that you've stayed at a party too long? That's when I decided it was time to take a powder. I did thank her for the drinks. It's not like I'm a cad or anything.

I stopped at the chicken place on my way home. My little blonde Rio was working the counter. But when I got into her line, some teen dork opened up a new register and asked if he could help me. I didn't want to appear suspect, so I just put my order in with dorkboy while stealing glances over at the blonde. I think her acne's clearing up. She's really turning into a woman.

I ordered half a chicken, rice and potatoes. Lots of starch to soak up the alcohol. I shouldn't have had that much to drink. I must have bought a pack of smokes at the bar, because I found a nearly full one in my pocket when I got home.

After murdering several people in Texas, including Lily Daltry who got two bullets to the back of her head for her trouble, Henry Lee Lucas claims he joined a cult called the Hand of Death. Since the cult believed that acts of perversion would help reincarnate the Devil, group leaders encouraged sodomy, sadomasochism and necrophilia following each Black Mass.

Lucas told of sacrifices of kidnapped children or traitors performed on an altar inside a sacred circle. He told of rituals involving eating their flesh and drinking their blood.

None of this was ever substantiated. It doesn't mean it wasn't true, though.

However, a number of tattoos Henry Lee Lucas received while he was a member of the cult mysteriously vanished on the day he turned to Christianity.

Or so he says.

Henry Lee Lucas' first victim was his mother. They had an argument and she struck him. He hit her back and she fell to the ground. It was then he realized, to his alleged surprise, that he had been holding a knife at the time.

His last victim was his thirteen-year-old common law wife, Becky, a sexy minx who had been used as an accomplice in several of his murders by luring strange men with promises of sex. In a fit of sudden uncontrollable rage, Henry Lee stabbed her in the chest on the day she told him she was leaving. Becky was the only woman he ever truly loved.

Or so he says.

I'm going to finish this chicken and take a quick nap. After that, I'm heading down to Mission V. for another look at 404 Winter Lane.

The flashing red light outside of the bar. It reminded me of something. Something I saw.

The Caddy.

Now I'm pretty sure I know how to find my way into the house.

TEN

Dear Diary,

She struggled. They always struggle.

But I'm getting way ahead of myself now.

Last night I overslept and didn't end up leaving my apartment until a little past midnight. I was still tired, but also very excited, too. It was show time and I had nearly an hour's drive ahead of me to paste my game face on.

Zero traffic, I made it down to Mission Viejo in fifty minutes.

404 Winter Lane was dark, as I had suspected. I drove away from the house, parked a couple of blocks down and walked back with my kit. This time I also brought a small nylon dog lead. Just in case someone starts getting nosy. I can always tell them I was walking my cockapoo and he got off his leash.

Hide under the veil of manipulated sympathy then vanish before anyone can figure it out. Magicians and con artists do it all the time.

There she is, I thought to myself as I gazed upon the Caddy sitting in the driveway. I peeked inside again. Bingo. The alarm indicator winking back at me like a tiny glowing red eye.

When the car alarm went off in the driveway, it took Bronwyn Baker less than one minute to get out of bed, turn on the lights, peek outside and then run downstairs to shut it off and then give the car a once-over to make sure it was okay.

In between the moment she deactivated the house alarm from inside to go outside and when she came back in and reactivated it, I pried open one of the living room windows around back.

And as Bronwyn Baker went back upstairs to bed, I crouched in the dark, wearing my black ski mask so I couldn't be seen. I heard her grumble the words: "Damn kids". Immediately I wondered angrily if that was the same thing she muttered under her breath as she held her children one by one underneath the surface of the water.

From above, I watched the bedroom light go out with a snap of the bedside lamp. There I sat, in the dark, trying not to breathe heavily as to be heard, trying to sit so that my stomach wouldn't grumble from hunger.

I sat and waited for forty-five minutes, timed perfectly to be the duration of half a REM cycle, the deepest moment of sleep.

Quietly, I crept across the carpeted floor and made my way up the steps. I moved very slowly, feeling with my right hand in front of me in the dark to make sure I wouldn't bump into anything.

As I reached the top of the steps, I let my eyes adjust to the darkness before proceeding. To my left was an open bedroom, a child's room, empty. To my left was another, also with no one occupying the neatly made bed.

While I crept toward the third bedroom door, I held my breath as to not make a sound. From my left hand, I could feel the kinetic energy of the heavy roll of duct tape just begging to be used.

Bronwyn Baker's snoring caught my ears even before I stepped into her room. After exhaling slowly, I snagged the exposed corner of the duct tape with the gloved fingers of my right hand. I took a deep breath and entered.

Even in the dim light from outside, I could see the outline of her body clearly. Her body stirred as I rushed into the room, turning toward me as I ripped a strip of duct tape as wide as my chest from the roll. Immediately, I could see her eyes pop open as I pushed it across her mouth, smoothing it flat from cheek to cheek. Her hands tried to come up from underneath the blankets to push me away, but I slapped her in the face, hard. The stunning blow gave her pause, which was the idea. A show of force up front to paralyze her with fear long enough for me to gain complete control of the situation. Mentacide. The act of destroying one's will through dominating their mind.

Her eyes were wide with fear and I could tell she could see me well enough in the dark because when I shook my head letting her know not to move, she responded with a small and very frightened nod.

I wound the duct tape around her wrists and then her ankles in total silence and she didn't even try to move at all. Her body was as rigid as stone.

When I was done, I went and looked closely at her face. I could now see her shaking as I came closer.

I peeled back the duct tape as I asked her what the alarm code was. I could smell the halitosis on her breath as she gave me a four-digit number. I put the tape back. But I wanted to make sure it wasn't a duress code alerting the cops there was an intruder in the house, so I took the box cutter from my pocket and grabbed her wrists. I pried her right pinky free and bent it back until I heard the snap of it breaking.

Her muffled shriek startled me a bit and I held the blade up to her wet eye and told her to be quiet. I pulled the tape back from her lips, expecting her to scream again but she didn't. I asked her what the alarm code was. She gave me the same number again. I was satisfied.

"Do you know why I'm here?" I whispered as I put the tape back. She shook her head. I could see her right hand was swelling up.

I turned and exited the bedroom. I went across the hall into the bathroom. I turned on the light. I turned on the water in the bathtub.

And when I came back into the bedroom, Bronwyn Baker was sobbing.

This is where she tried to fight me. She brought up her duct-taped hands as one fist and hammered on my chest until I threw her onto the floor. I grabbed the blanket from the bed and wrapped her in it like a cocoon as I wound the duct tape around her. Then I dragged her across the floor and into the bathroom. I could hear my joints pop as I bent down to lift her up.

"This is for your babies," I whispered to her, though I don't know if she could hear me over the roar of running water.

And when I dropped her into the bathtub, the same one where she had taken the lives of her own children, the water overflowed onto the floor and onto my shoes as she sank right to the bottom.

The air bubbles from her scream surfaced up from under the duct tape covering her mouth. As she lay there on the bottom of the tub, our eyes connected, quite deeply in fact. And in there for that small moment I could see her sorrow, I could see her regret. Call me crazy, but in her eyes was an act of contrition.

I don't know what came over me at that moment but I reached down into the water and grabbed a handful of the blanket she was wrapped in. All at once, I pulled her out of the tub and dropped her onto the floor and walked out of there as fast as I could.

But as I passed one of the empty bedrooms in the hallway, I paused. I entered and switched on the light. On the wall were baseball pennants and posters. On the dresser, a globe sat next to an empty fish tank. There on the desk next to me was a framed photo of a beaming young boy in his little league uniform. The boy who should have been in the room's tiny twin bed dreaming of pop flies and ice cream was gone and never coming back.

I put the photo back on the desk and went back into the bathroom.

Bronwyn Baker was still there on the wet floor breathing heavily through her nose. I didn't say anything. I just picked her up. This time, she wriggled like hell and fought me all the way into the water.

And as she struggled against the binds that would never come off, I went back into her bedroom to look for something. When I came back, I was carrying a small hand mirror I'd found on her dresser. I held it up just over the surface of the water so that Bronwyn Baker could watch herself die.

My arms grew tired from holding the mirror but I kept it there for ten minutes even though I knew her still open eyes weren't seeing anything anymore.

Downstairs, I found my knapsack in the living room where I had left it. I slipped out of the wet clothes I had on and stuffed them into a trash bag I'd brought before getting into some dry sweats.

I punched in the alarm code she'd twice given me and watched the indicator light go green. Then I opened the door and left.

And all of Winter Lane in Mission Viejo slept quietly as I walked back to my car and drove away.

But it was a few seconds later that I was hit by a shock that caused me to slam on my brakes. I had turned the radio up and was taking off my rubber gloves when I noticed it. A raisin-sized hole in the latex exposing part of my right index finger tip.

Dear Diary,

Woke up when the alarm went off. Very tired this morning. Did twenty-five sit-ups before my head started throbbing. Needed a painkiller, so I took two Binafan and washed them down in the shower with water from the showerhead. Running late. Fried egg sandwich on wheat for breakfast. Took only one bite. No appetite.

Zero news about Red or about Bronwyn Baker. Teacher's strike apparently settled last night. Looks very likely that the kids will be back in school by the end of the week.

Got to work a few minutes early to find that The Fossil was already there. One of the receptionists up front told me he had blown in like a dry old tumbleweed a half hour before. I wanted to tell her I didn't care.

Whiney-Ass found me in the break room pouring myself a cup of coffee and asked if I was worried.

"'Bout what?" I responded.

"About losing your job!" he nearly yelled in my face as if I were some kind of numbskull. My head was still throbbing. I was thinking about the rip in my glove. During the whole drive home, I kept going over in my mind how it could have happened, and then it hit me.

The moment I rushed Bronwyn Baker's bed and pulled that duct tape off the roll.

I have a feeling the sticky part of the tape took the tiny bit of my fingertip with it.

I was about to drive back to her house to find it but I had a feeling it was at the bottom of her bathtub. Fingerprints don't do so well in water, the oils dissolve quickly. I decided a return trip wasn't worth the risk.

I had touched the hand-held mirror, too but had dropped that into the tub as well.

Come morning, I was feeling a bit sick about it. I kept thinking about going back down there tonight, but I didn't have a key, and going in through the window again would instantly set off her alarm.

Whiney-Ass was still talking about a rumor he'd heard about outsourcing. His lips were moving and sounds were coming out, but it was like he was speaking Farsi or something. Only every third word registered with me. I told him I thought I was going to be sick and walked out without my coffee.

I went outside to grab a smoke. Obviously, I wasn't the only one feeling the stress because there were many more people than usual, all standing out there nervously sucking back on their cancer sticks.

My hands were shaking as I lit up my cigarette. I checked my pack. Only a half dozen left. Probably not enough to get through the workday.

"Hi," she said, and I looked up to find Miss Big Nose, arms folded and looking concerned.

"It's never a good sign when the whole H.R. department gets called into a meeting," she whispered, referring to the cabal in the big conference room. "I heard they were talking about fighting off a hostile takeover. You know that never ends well for the company getting swallowed."

"You know what I hate about H.R.?" I told her. "You have a bunch of people who are supposedly looking out for your welfare, but they're paid by the company to maximize the cost-benefit ratio of your job. Seems like a classic conflict of interest to me."

Apparently, I'd said it a bit too loud because some other people looked at me. Fuck 'em. I don't care.

"Sorry about having to take off so soon the other night," I said softly so only she could hear. I could still imagine her tongue in my mouth and her drunken hands on my crotch and where it all seemed to be headed.

She just gave me a look. But there was a strange intimacy about it. More like an invasive quality. It was a look like she knew something about me, and I wasn't sure if I liked it.

I pretended I had forgotten to call back a customer and left, wondering exactly what I was going to have to do with Miss Big Nose, if she really did know too much about me.

ELEVEN

Dear Diary,

I'm pretty sure this was somehow meant to happen. Last night, I went out for drinks with Trina—a.k.a. Miss Big Nose —and we ended up in bed together. Let me say that I must have had my head up my ass all this time, because I had no idea what a little slut she was. I think I spent so much effort trying to keep a low profile at the office that I never really even contemplated it, or her for that matter.

Though the whole thing may have come about because of what a clusterfuck things have become this week at work. It's like Stockholm Syndrome. Except we're both hostages to a job we hate. But isn't that the way of the world anymore?

Birth. School. Work. Death.

Every day, upper management had been seen together in meeting after meeting, huddled together to trade shifty-eyed whispers of some unforeseen future path to be taken and when I wasn't out servicing clients, it seemed like I was out in the smoking area with half the people who work here consuming gossip.

This person was supposedly getting fired. That department was going to be outsourced to India.

Every day, it was something different. I swear, I think there were people taking up smoking just so they could be out there to hear the latest dope. It really made me kind of glad I hadn't quit yet. It seemed like more often than not, every time I'd be out there, Trina would be too. It even got to the point that I'd go search her out at her desk or she'd come to mine beforehand. We had moved into that moderately comfortable territory reserved for smoke buddies.

Then, yesterday, we were out there discussing the latest rumor, how The Fossil was going to turn the reins of the company over to his idiot son who would most likely run the whole thing into the ground much like the Minor League baseball team he had once owned. Suddenly her fingers touched my arm and she asked if I wanted to meet for a drink after work at the same dive bar from the other night.

I said sure.

Turns out that later they called everybody into the big conference room to make a few announcements and we really had something to drink about.

So, yes, we got hammered, and yes, we ended up back in the parking lot with our hands all over each other, the whole time Trina saying a couple of the girls at work were talking about how she and I had been seen having hushed private conversations off to the side.

Finally, she asked if I wanted to go to her place and fuck. You have to love single older women; they just cut to the chase.

I followed her in my car and parked next to her. We pawed each other all the way to the door. Once inside, she started talking real dirty like how she wanted me to pin her arms above her head up against the wall and tear her panties off. So I did. And when I reached under her skirt, she was soaked and wasn't even wearing panties, but she wanted me to pretend I was tearing them off. I unbuttoned her blouse with one hand while I held her wrists together with the other and then she pushed me against the other wall and attacked my neck so hard I thought she was giving me a hickey.

She pulled me down on top of her as we fell onto the couch and she undid my pants as I reached up under her bra. When I pulled it off her, I noticed she had gigantic dark nipples, and she put both hands on my ass as I was trying to shake off my left shoe, and she guided me inside of her.

"I'm on the pill," she whispered to me as my cock split her lips, and I tried to push the thought of how many guys she may have said that to out of my head.

Whether she faked it or not, she came hard and it got me excited. When I was done, she wanted more. I was feeling the effects of the booze. I'm not the young man I used to be. She took me into her bedroom and I watched as she took a vibrator from her dresser and toyed with her clit until she came again. As I got hard again, I wanted her to climb on top of me and ride me. I had a feeling she would fuck me through the mattress. She didn't want to. She only wanted me on top of her.

I was a bit annoyed but wasn't about to look a gift pussy in the mouth, if that even makes sense.

Holding out as long as I could seemed like forever, and when I started to actually get sore, I pulled out and came on her belly.

After a cigarette, I went into her bathroom and took a shower. Not because I normally do that kind of thing, but because I really needed to be alone with my thoughts for a few minutes and away from her.

I pulled back the plastic curtain (clear with yellow ducks, baby blue liner) and stepped inside while the warm water fell onto my face. I could still smell her on my fingers so I washed myself all over with soap and as I watched the suds go down the drain, I realized Trina's tub was the same tan color as Bronwyn Baker's.

When I got out, I left the water running while I checked her medicine cabinet. I worked with a guy years ago who told me of a one-night stand he had with a girl he picked up at a club, went back to her place, fucked and fell asleep. The next morning, all hungover, he went to look for an aspirin and found she had three different kinds of prescription medication for foot fungus.

I asked him if he had sucked her toes. He said he wasn't sure, he was really drunk.

Nothing in Trina's medicine cabinet other than Band-Aids, disposable razor blades, cold and flu medication and an earwax removal kit. No prescriptions.

I realized later she probably hides them in a drawer.

The third time we did it, (missionary... again) I tried to put her knees up on my shoulders. She told me it hurt, so I put them back down. I grabbed her hair pretty hard and she didn't care for that either. She actually cried out a little, which actually didn't excite me as much as I thought it would. I must have been tired.

Finally, we fell asleep. I woke up a couple of hours later when her cat jumped on the bed. I thought someone had broken in and was about to try to kill whatever had startled me in my stupor when I heard the soft metallic jangle of its collar. It started purring like it wanted me to pet it. It's not that I don't like cats. I just wasn't in the mood. But it stuck its wet nose in my face and I stroked its neck for a minute until it jumped off me.

When the morning came, Trina offered breakfast (ready-pour pancakes from a container and turkey bacon, yuck). I made an excuse that I was meeting a buddy to help him move his pool table, so he could clean his rugs for a party. Pulled that one out of my ass. I can't begin to wonder where that even came from.

Truth was she didn't look half as bad as I feared she would in the light of morning. Still, I wasn't about to stick around for pancakes and chit-chat.

I got in my car, and it still smelled a bit like shit. I was very glad I hadn't eaten anything.

When I got home, I lay down on the couch and slept for another hour. Then I got up and checked my e-mail and started to feel sick.

I had two messages from Eddy.

The cops had found Bronwyn Baker. She didn't show up for work and the police made a welfare call on her house. He said they found the pry marks I'd left outside the living room window, so they broke the lock to get in.

It was dark. I was working as fast as possible.

He said she didn't look so good after three days in the tub.

Makes me wonder if he was actually there or saw a photo. But there was no attachment to the e-mail.

My balls crawled into my gut when I opened the second e-mail.

In the first sentence he asked me if I had anything to do with the dead hooker that was found in the Valley up by the 118 freeway.

I racked my brain to remember if I had maybe mentioned it to him. I had thought about it, just in case, to give him a heads up. Even the nights I was drunk.

I hadn't told anyone.

My hands were shaking. I read the rest of the e-mail. He said there had been one eyewitness report of a car stopped at the culvert for a couple of minutes. The description was vague, but matched mine exactly.

I got up from the computer and started pacing the floor trying to figure out how to respond. My first inclination was to tell him about what I had done to Red, so he could keep an eye out for me. But there was something bothering me. A little tiny voice deep down inside was telling me that I still had to be very careful about trusting Eddy, about what I told him.

He had given me Bronwyn Baker's address and a small bit of background on her. He hadn't told me how to go about it.

I sat down to write that I had done Red on my way back from staking out 404 Winter Lane on his suggestion, but then got up from the keyboard and began pacing again.

I was just being led around like a lapdog. He had sent me off to square away Tito Gomez, but had hardly mentioned what was going on with the case. The guy had been mutilated and burned. I couldn't believe the cops weren't all over that one.

And what about the latent print on his trunk lid? What was going on with that?

The more I thought about it, the more I started to think there was something rotten about this whole thing.

Pacing more, I chain-smoked two cigarettes while I went over different ways to vaguely word my response.

But then I realized the best course of action would be to not put anything incriminating at all into an e-mail. I hit reply and told Eddy I had to talk to him in person.

After clicking send, I sat there and stared at my inbox for an hour, constantly refreshing my screen over and over. I was hoping he would respond quickly. He didn't.

Finally, I gave up. I started thinking about the possibility of getting rid of my car. It wasn't like I could afford to buy a new one or even take on a bigger car payment, especially with all the uncertainty at work.

I thought about going down to Earl Sheib and getting a cheap paint job, but then, that itself would be something people would notice. I contemplated the possibility of getting into a car accident, but that would also bring more attention, and would raise my premiums.

Hell, a lot of people have the same car I do. Nobody was going to pull me over because I was driving it.

But if suspicion drew closer, it would be another detail the cops would notice.

I went back and checked my e-mail again. Nothing. Other than more junk from that Nigerian prince offering to move ninety million dollars through my account.

Now that's a guy I could probably kill and get a fucking medal for it.

It was really getting to me. I kept refreshing the page every two seconds and I realized I would probably lose my mind if I didn't just get the fuck out of there.

I refreshed the page again.

And again.

And now I'm just going to grab my keys and go. Eddy, you had better write me back.

TWELVE

Dear Diary,

Today is my first day without a cigarette.

Bad night last night. No sleep. I was exhausted when I got back.

When I left yesterday I drove, not caring where I was going. Just got behind the wheel and ate concrete.

I found myself up on the 405 with the need to get out of the car. Like it was some kind of coffin.

I got off at Santa Monica Boulevard and went west. Turned north up into the residential area all the way up Barrington toward Wilshire and parked. I was restless like I had been caged, so I decided to schlep the three-plus miles down to the oceanfront in Santa Monica. I needed to take the air and clear my head. It was starting to throb, to rat-a-tat-tat like a Gene Krupa drum solo.

Those thoughts, bouncing around in my head like a million little rubber balls colliding against the walls of my skull trying to get out. I could almost actually feel them buzzing around, like if I tilted my ear to the ground they would all come rushing out, spilling all around me.

I started down the sidewalk, past the Pavilions grocery store, past a homeless guy walking around carrying a refrigerator box on his head.

I suppose among bums that qualifies as a mobile home.

I made it past the China Dragon, which had a letter grade of "C" hanging in the window courtesy of the L.A. Health Commissioner's office, before my thoughts even started to come together in my mind.

Eddy had asked if I was the one who killed the hooker and as I was trying to think of anything else, I couldn't help but remember that moment in the car with Red when I had rammed that screwdriver blade through the back of her neck and into her cerebral cortex. When I picked her up, I hadn't planned on killing her, at least not consciously. It had just happened on impulse like the way you pick up a candy bar or some Tic Tacs while in line at the supermarket. It just seemed to me like if God hadn't intended for hookers to be murdered so easily he wouldn't have put them right there in harm's way. I dunno.

The more I tried to figure out what had triggered it, the more I kept thinking it had been a number of things. I had been frustrated about driving all the way down to Mission V. I had been annoyed at not finding anything for my trouble. It had been a spur of the moment decision that felt like it had been made outside of my own body, and the next thing I knew she was bleeding from her brain and shitting herself in my car. I ended her life because she was pathetic, something less than human to me. And somewhere deep down inside I had heard a small voice telling me she would be better off dead than alive. A whisper telling me that by taking her life, I was sparing her another day of enduring the sheer pain of living as a piece of street scum.

I passed the grimy pet store with the grimy turtles in the window. I walked by an Italian restaurant that smelled like garbage. I nearly bumped into some drunken fucker stumbling through the front door of some bar called The Shack.

And for that one slight moment, I imagined what the drunk's expression would look like if I had turned and buried a knife into his gut instead of walking away.

There was no doubt I was in a state of some kind—like a powder keg. I thought of turning back and going into The Shack and getting a beer to take the edge off, but then started picturing a moment where the same drunk bumps into me again, where I lose it, break my beer bottle and carve a flap into his face with the jagged edge. I could see it all too clear in my head as if it were being projected onto the back wall of my skull by my eyes. Pushing him against the wall, catching him off balance, jamming the sharp glass into his eye socket and turning clockwise across his forehead.

I kept walking. I kept walking.

Past the hospital and the crummy movie house that only shows the kind of films that pseudo-intellectual douchebags sit around and discuss over cups of hot Darjeeling tea brewed in a French press.

As I got to Third Street, near the Promenade, I could see the girls. A half dozen of them, all dressed in the same style of teenage slutwear. Standing around text messaging on their phones, probably to each other.

Half of them wore belly shirts but had no business in them, which seems to be the rage. One of them caught me staring as I passed and gave me a dirty look. My eyes may have been on her, but my mind wasn't.

I could almost hear the sound that screwdriver made, like a knife slicing through the skin of a cucumber.

Finally, I got to the ocean. My dogs were barking something fierce, so I took a seat on a bench at the park high atop the bluff overlooking PCH. There, a homeless man with matted black hair and a face like a collapsed lung alternated between playing an out-of-tune acoustic guitar and using it for a pillow.

My attention was drawn to the Ferris wheel there on the pier. Having never been on one, I sat transfixed, watching the gigantic spokes turn. I remember the carnival mom took me to the second summer after dad died and she told me she was too afraid of heights to go on the rinky-dink Ferris wheel, so we rode the carousel three times instead. I hated the fucking thing. My dad never would have taken me on the carousel.

How did Eddy know about Red? Did he just get lucky and guess? That wouldn't be like him at all.

What is his game?

I sat there for an hour watching the Ferris wheel go around and, not coming up with answers, decided to head back. I thought of the long walk to my car and resolved not to put it off any more. As I approached The Shack, I crossed the street to the other side on the off chance the same drunk came tumbling out into me again. There was no doubt what I would have done to him.

I passed the big liquor store and stopped in for a small bag of cashews and a soda ($4.59). The clerk spoke to me in a language I didn't understand and when I made a face to let him know that, he apologized and said I looked like someone else he knew.

Everybody says that about me.

As I got up to the corner of Wilshire and Bundy Drive, I thought of how one of America's most famous double homicides happened on a street with the same exact name as one of America's most infamous serial murderers. A block up, I passed the McDonalds where O.J. and Kato had their final meal together the night his wife and the dude fucking her ended up nearly decapitated.

Once, maybe a year ago, I had walked the mile or so up to Nicole Brown Simpson's condo. They had since remodeled the outside as to be less noticeable, since in L.A. you can pay some dirtbag to give you a driving death tour in a nice air-conditioned van. Nicole's condo, the house where Marylin Monroe overdosed herself on a barbiturate suppository, the John Holmes Wonderland murders location. All there to enjoy. Ticket please.

The new owners had put in a wall and terra cotta entryway to keep the looky-loos away, but I'd known which place to look for. They even changed the address from 875 to 879 S. Bundy Drive. Though many years had passed since the event that transformed this neighborhood, I could feel him here, O.J. wearing a mask and gloves, trying to escape as his Bruno Maglis left behind a bloody footprint. I imagined him big, though slowed by age. I imagined silently slipping behind him as he left through the back gate into the alley; looping the piano wire garrote over his neck and pulling tightly on the wooden handles I had tied the ends to. As he fell, I would incapacitate him by stomping on the side of one of his injured knees, feeling the old joint shatter like a Christmas ornament. As he struggled for breath, I'd push him down to the ground and yank tight on the garrote while putting a knee into his back and driving his face hard enough into the pavement to break cartilage and bone. Having just killed two people, he would have been high on adrenaline, but most likely out of breath. With one sharp yank on the garrote, I would bring the piano wire slicing into his neck like the thin metal strings of an egg cutter.

I imagined leaving his head nearly severed and dropping the garrote but taking one look inside the gate of the condo before leaving. There I would step over the dead young man on the ground and go over to Nicole, curled up in the fetal position in the courtyard, lying in a thick pool of her and Goldman's blood. I would tell her how sorry I was that I couldn't have gotten there ten minutes earlier. After kissing my fingertips, I'd lay them on her cheek before vanishing into the night.

There was part of me that wanted to trek up to 879 S. Bundy—that maybe there was an answer to be had to my questions. My feet still hurt and I was anxious to get back to my place to deal with what was waiting for me there.

I could feel the heaviness in my chest. I still hadn't figured out how to respond to Eddy's e-mail. To keep my mind off it, I tried thinking about what had happened with Trina. Her nearly pathological insistence of only using the missionary position even though we had fucked three times. What was she afraid of? That I'd see the unsightly ripples of cellulite on her ass if I'd taken her from behind? What do I care as long as I'm getting laid?

And then as I thought about it more and how it annoyed me she wouldn't let me do her doggy style, I started to wonder if she had been afraid in some way of having me behind her, of not being able to see me.

Again I recalled the look she had given me the other day outside in the smoking area at work—the gaze that felt like a scalpel cutting into my skin. It was no accident. When a woman gives you that kind of look for that long, she's telling you something. She wants you to know she knows something about you.

What was that she had said that first night in the bar? That people were going to think I was the Interstate Slasher? Why the fuck would she say that?

What does she know?

Is it sheer coincidence that she's been trying to get close to me since Tito Gomez? The day she followed me into the break room. That was right after I'd come back.

Who does she know? Is there a connection between her and Eddy?

Is he having me watched? Is he having me followed? He knew

I'd be going down to Mission V. on the night he sent me that e-mail to check out 404 Winter Lane.

How difficult would it have been to tail me? Not once had I even thought to carefully check my rear-view mirror. I thought of my stop at the burger joint and the mongoloid kid ordering six packs of cookies. There had been another guy there in line. (Blond hair, glasses, maybe six-two-ish). I hadn't given him much notice.

Was that Eddy?

How else would he know I had killed the hooker that night if I hadn't been tailed?

Did I think to watch if I was being followed when Red was dying in my car? No. I'd been too busy panicking over where to dump her.

I got in my car and drove, barely paying attention. I made it back to my front door, fumbling my keys as my brain tried to process more questions than answers.

As I got inside, I went into the bathroom and locked the door. I sat on the floor with my back to the wall. It came to me that if I was being watched, the last thing I could do was let them know I knew. I splashed water in my face and went back to my computer.

Eddy's e-mail was still open. His question asking if I had anything to do with the dead hooker up by the 118 still staring me in the face.

I realized there was nothing else I could do but wait. I had to keep up appearances. For some reason, it seemed strange to have to think about what I would be doing if I hadn't been so self-conscious about it. In my mind, a laundry list of the things I normally do reeled back and forth.

I took my cell phone into the bathroom and jerked off to the pictures of the hot teenage girls I'd taken in the mall in Vegas. I was just going through the motions. As I came, I didn't even enjoy it.

I decided to go to the chicken place to get dinner. Rio, my little blonde, was there and that helped me take my mind off things. As I ordered my two-piece (white meat with steamed carrots and coleslaw) I asked her how it was going. She smiled at me and told me it was going alright. Call me crazy, but just for a moment, there was a connection.

And then just like that, it was gone.

As I sat in the back, at a table facing the counter, I stole glances at her, the way her breasts pushed up against her uniform top. I bit into my chicken and thought of how it would feel to pin her against a wall and rub my hard-on against the crotch of her polyester pants.

My fantasy was struck dead when my cell phone rang. It was an unlisted number. When I answered, the person on the other end hung up.

Right then, I happened to look out the window. There was a car pulling away. One I thought had come from the drive-thru, but wasn't positive.

But it sure drove by slowly enough to make me wonder.

THIRTEEN

Dear Diary,

Four days, no cigarette. Quite possibly because I've gotten a blowjob from Trina each one of those days. Three times during lunch in her car and once out back behind the office building before hours—which, in my honest opinion, was a bit forced and rushed. During the workday, we hardly make eye contact with each other because claims it would be a big hassle if anybody in the office found out we had taken our relationship past that cordial work politeness of superficially asking how one was doing or if the kids were well.

I agreed. Mostly because the natural assumption of most people would lean towards some kind of relationship, and as far as I could tell we were just fucking.

She said if H.R. ever found out we'd have to fill out paperwork. I told her paperwork was a tool of Satan to prevent mortal productivity and I would burn in hell if I even tried contemplating what she had just said.

Then I told her I thought that she was in H.R. She informed me she was in charge of consolidation of deliverables. Something came out of my mouth about how important her job sounded. I could tell by her puckered cat-butt expression that she knew my words were as sincere as a whoopee cushion. This was just shortly after I had come in her mouth in the front seat of her Nissan.

Honestly, I think she gets off on all this cloak and dagger shit because there is nothing else in her life other than an empty apartment and a cat.

But I get to unload in her throat or on her face almost every day, so I'm not about to kill the goose that lays the golden blowjob, even if every time she goes down on me her big nose pokes annoyingly into my groin.

Subtly, I have been trying to get her to reveal if she knows more than she leads on.

On Monday, as she pulled her hair back and lowered her face into my lap, I told her I was afraid of cops coming by and seeing us. Momentarily, she took her mouth off me and said that I needed to, in her words, live dangerously.

Does that mean anything? Probably not.

After lunch today, I was informed that my supervisor, the Lipless Wonder, had been given a severance package. He and a half dozen people in lower-middle management were let go.

Let the culling begin.

I avoided Trina on the way out of the office today. I had been listening to one of my customers drone on about some of the features on the PDX-2000 he was hoping would be improved with a firmware update, when I remembered something that John Wayne Gacy had done to several of his victims.

He had tricked them into putting on a pair of handcuffs.

It was simple, really. He had dressed up like a clown for kids' birthdays, neighborhood parties and nursing home visits. He'd deftly whip out a couple of magic tricks and make people laugh. He conned his victims, often young men lured to his home with promises of booze and sex, into actually putting the cuffs onto themselves believing it was some kind of entertainment.

And it had been, at least for Gacy. The entertainment had come as he looped a rope around their necks and twisted it with a piece of wood until he strangled them. Sometimes into semi-consciousness so he could have sex with them, only to revive them and strangle them again—in many cases, for hours at a time as their throats burned with insufferable pain and the pleading for their own lives went ignored.

Gacy had been, for all intents and purposes, a normal guy. He had been a pillar of the community. One time when First Lady Roslyn Carter had come to visit the city of Chicago, Gacy had been chosen to show her around. He had been named Jaycee man of the year in three different cities. He was a successful building contractor. In the winter, he shoveled walkways for elderly neighbors and decorated his house with elaborate Christmas lights. John Wayne Gacy was so well-loved that when his wife and mother-in-law complained to him about the continuing horrible smell of decay wafting up from the basement and he told them it was from rats that had crawled in between the walls and died, they believed him and never questioned it again.

Went to lunch today with Whiney-Ass and a guy I can't stand who I will only refer to as The Tool. Lunch buffet at Sonny Chow's ($7.99).

The Tool just rubs me the wrong way. If Whiney-Ass is sandpaper against my nerves, the Tool is a dentist's drill against the pulpy root of a molar. Though he works in the tech writing department creating and updating product manuals, he thinks he knows exactly how the entire world is run—the tired m.o. of every complete and total jackass.

While chomping loudly on an eggroll, he proceeded to tell us how the global financial crisis caused by the big 1995 earthquake in Kobe, Japan and the fall of the Nikkei ultimately caused the World Trade Center attacks. Then he spent ten excruciating minutes spouting off on how our jobs are in jeopardy because ten years ago the Fossil switched suppliers from Japan to cheaper ones in China but that several quarterly write downs due to shoddy manufacturing ultimately cost the company millions in lost revenue. I started getting douche chills just thinking of stabbing him with a chopstick.

Whiney-Ass had The Tool tell the story of how he had gotten wasted at a buddy's bachelor send-off at some bar in Carpinteria and picked up this hot drunk girl.

He said they went back to her place and she wanted it doggy style in the ass all night long.

This was while I was trying to eat my Broccoli Beef.

Then he said he woke up hours later in her bed, still a bit drunk, grabbed his hard-on and then realized when he couldn't feel it that it wasn't his. She had a dick.

"At least it wasn't as big as mine," he laughed. He boasted how he was going to write it up real nice and submit it to dirtytrannystories.com. Whiney-Ass guffawed and nearly spit a steamed dumpling across the table. As the two of them high-fived, a pair of blue-haired grandmas sitting nearby gave us dagger stares.

Honestly, it got to the point where I very much had to hold back from stabbing The Tool in the throat just to get him to shut the fuck up.

"You know the slaughter isn't over," The Tool said as we split the check. "Management's gonna let more people go."

Dear Diary,

Friday morning. Woke up early to the sound of a garbage truck. I was hugging my knees in the fetal position. My back feels a bit achy. Did fifty pushups. Showered. Wheat toast and a banana for breakfast. I read where the potassium makes your semen taste sweeter. Thought I'd try it out— throw Trina a bone.

So to speak.

Light blue short sleeve button-down shirt. Tan slacks. Black socks. Black shoes. Office camouflage. Don't want to be too conspicuous.

Airplane tragedy on the radio. Passenger jet went down in the Caspian Sea near Kazakhstan or Kurdistan—one of the Stans. Another recall of toys made in China. Grocery workers strike averted for now.

Still no call or e-mail from Eddy. I sent him another message asking if he got my last one. Must play it cool.

Arrived at work early for my morning Big Nose Knob Shine. All this week, her car was here before mine. Today, I waited twenty minutes for her to show before throwing in the towel

The new policy at the office is to sign in and out at the front desk. Every morning, they now take attendance, so it feels like high school but without any of the fun of farting in class. After I scribbled my name, I checked the other sheets on the sign-in clipboard; Trina definitely hadn't come in yet. New girl behind the front desk. Thin and pretty. Poker straight dark hair. (Red pullover blouse, frilly collar, gold cross around her neck.) Those big blue corn-fed eyes make her look like she just got off the bus from Kansas.

I schlepped to my desk to get an early start on figuring out a new system of sales reporting. After five minutes, all the words on the electronic form started to blur together. But then, when I tried to open my browser to kill a few minutes reading the new posts in the independent provider feedback forum on theeroticreview.com, the page had been blocked.

I tried some more sites. Blocked.

Amazon, blocked. Yahoo, blocked.

Dirtytrannystories.com, blocked.

On my way to the break room for coffee, I almost expected to find searchlights sweeping across the tops of the cubicles.

Fresh pot of joe on the burner. That much at least was going for me. I poured myself one and absently flipped through a newspaper someone had left on the table. U.S. Men's Gymnastics team comes in second in world championships. Yawn.

Historical building in downtown L.A. burns down. Yawn. In L.A. what does that mean? It was built in the 1930s. Gimme a break.

Papua, New Guinea, AIDS victims being buried alive.

Now that's a story.

Hermosa Beach, CA. Paroled sex offender arrested taking photos near schoolyard. In some countries, they would have castrated this guy.

Ten years before his arrest for killing a fifteen year-old boy named Robert Piest, John Wayne Gacy had been working as a manager of a Kentucky Fried Chicken restaurant owned by his first father-in-law. During this time he was convicted of handcuffing and sodomizing one of his juvenile male employees.

It's terrible. Honestly though, it could have been Gacy's way of training this kid for what the real corporate workplace is like.

I joke, but it's true.

Who knows? Maybe the kid asked for a raise?

After police searched the crawlspace under Gacy's house, they found the decomposed remains of twenty-eight boys between the ages of fifteen and twenty. Some so skeletized and putrefied cause of death or positive identification would never be known. Others still with ropes tied around their necks or wads of cloth stuffed down their esophaguses probably to keep them from bleeding on Gacy's floor.

There had been one guy who had managed to survive his encounter with Gacy. After having a chloroform-soaked rag clamped over his face, this young man woke up naked in Gacy's house of horrors. Then for some unknown reason, after a night of whipping and raping him, Gacy let him go. Just like that. Thanks for coming.

And even though the guy went to the cops, nobody believed his wild story enough to get Gacy arrested.

There's a lesson to be learned here.

On the way back to my cubicle, I took a detour to Trina's desk to see if she was there. She wasn't. One of the busybody matrons nearby looked up at me like a bird from a feed dish. I continued and headed to the bathroom where I stood by the sink and examined my cuticles. The joints in my fingers were feeling a bit stiff as well. A quick peek in the mirror made me feel my age.

And as I walked back to my desk, it hit me.

The Interstate Slasher. Maybe he was quiet for four years because he had been incarcerated.

Fifty months is a long time to sit and plan. Or sit and fantasize.

If that's the case he had to have been serving time for something unrelated. Had there been an arrest for the Cupcake Lane murder, I would have known.

The idea buzzed inside my head like a hive of loose bees. I couldn't work. I was obsessed. I had to find out more about the Interstate Slasher. I had already gone through every one of his murders. Each body had been dumped at a different location than where the actual abduction and killing most likely took place. Second, he had taken his time with the victims. Third, he'd been very careful not to leave any traces of evidence on the body.

This guy had the classic earmarks of an anger-excitation killer. Someone who plans the rape, murder and disposal. Someone primarily motivated to inflict as much terror and pain on the victim as possible for his or her own sexual gratification.

Someone who would calmly tell their victim exactly how they were going to torture and rape them for days or weeks, before slowly killing them.

Fucking website blocker on the company internet was keeping me from looking up anything, so I got up from my desk and went outside. Not out back to the smoking area, out front to my car. I had to get me more info on the Interstate Slasher cases. Did he ejaculate? Were all the victims of a similar type? Long legs? Petite? Slutty? Anything.

I got inside my car. I had one number for Eddy. The one from which he had text messaged to give me the whereabouts of Tito Gomez. I called.

Number not in service. Fuck.

Eddy probably bought a pre-paid phone with cash and dumped it after using it to contact me.

I wanted to throw my phone across the parking lot. I got out of my car. Pissed.

And as I shut my door, that's when it started to ring. It was a number I didn't recognize.

I answered. It was Eddy.

He told me to get back into my car and drive. I told him I had to sign out of work. He said it couldn't wait.

So I drove.

Falling in behind me was a cargo van with a windshield so heavily tinted it looked like a bottomless void. Though I tried, I couldn't make out who was behind the wheel.

He said he only had a minute. I told him I was sure I discovered something about the Interstate Slasher. He said that would come in time. There was something more important. Before I could talk, he anticipated my first question.

"I was surveilling you to make sure nobody else was watching. I couldn't contact you until I knew it was safe to talk."

I nearly froze. What did the cops know?

Eddy continued, "Killing the whore was stupid and careless," he told me sharply and I could feel myself get hot as if he had just slapped me in the face.

"The eyewitness' name is Carl Bishop. Lives in the neighborhood. Guy's an insomniac. Was up walking his dog on a hill that overlooks where you dumped the body."

The first thing I asked was why I hadn't heard about any of this on the news.

"Two reasons," Eddy said. "First the lead detective on the case believes this might be the work of the Interstate Slasher..."

"What?" I exclaimed. I couldn't believe what I was hearing. "Are you kidding me? It's not the same m.o. It's not even the same kind of killing! The girl is wrong..."

"You know that. I know that. But some of these young guys, they all think there's one big case out there that'll be their ticket. Book deal. Larry King. Movie of the week. If this guy starts pointing fingers and yelling 'Interstate Slasher', then maybe he gets more resources from the department. More guys he can tell what to do."

From the tone of his voice, I could tell Eddy was nervous.

"Second," he said. "This Carl Bishop guy, turns out he's in the witness relocation program."

"You're shitting me," I said, still stunned.

"Swear," he responded. "Son of a bitch dropped dime on a couple of Cubano gangsters in Florida. Sketchy testimony in exchange for getting a new name and life."

And I knew right then and there it was going to be up to me to take that life away.

FOURTEEN

Dear Diary,

My temples throbbed and my entire head buzzed the whole drive home after work as I kept thinking about how, just for a moment, Eddy seemed nervous, how he sounded like the thin veneer of control had slipped away. When I tried to ask him if he had heard anything more about Bronwyn Baker or Tito Gomez, he said it would have to wait until later. What that meant was lost on me but it was bothersome, like a burr in my heel. He insisted we had to get off the phone, that it was too risky. I wanted to scream at him, but he said he'd call back soon and then bailed.

Click. Gone. Bye.

I looked at the now-silent phone in my hand, then turned around and drove back to work.

When I got back in, Miss Corn Fed at the front desk reminded me I had forgotten to sign out. I put on the old "aw shucks" routine coupled with a slight laugh.

"I can't remember all these new rules," I grinned as I picked up the clipboard.

"I won't tell anyone if you won't," she whispered out loud, and with it came a slight, yet meaningless smile before she turned back to the ringing phone.

B-cup. Definitely. Not bad.

I spent the rest of the day calling my customers, checking in, and shooting the shit. They like that. Some even think I'm their friend.

Pete, at one of the companies I visited in San Diego told me he was filing for divorce this week. I said I was sorry to hear that. He told me not to be. She didn't want kids. He did. It was a deal breaker for him.

"Besides," he told me. "She can't cook for shit. When she serves a meal it comes in one of two flavors, burnt or ptomaine."

Pete groused the divorce would cost him a bundle and she was enough of a bitch that she'd try to take the house.

"I'll kill her first," he said. "How hard would it be to drive twenty minutes and cross the border and find some shady guy in T.J. to do it for a couple grand?"

Honestly, I wasn't sure what to say. I'd met this palooka face to face once and I couldn't believe what he was telling me. What else was he dying to talk about? Cheating on his taxes? Injecting heroin into his scrote bag so nobody will see the track marks?

"I'm just kidding, man. Lighten up," he said, most likely misconstruing my silence as horror.

"No, I was doing the math in my head to see if it'd be worth a couple grand to take the job," I laughed, trying to steer the conversation away. "You know, gas prices these days and all."

"Hey, if you want it, it's yours," he replied, which made some of the hairs stand up on the back of my neck. Was this just male-bonding dude-talk or was Pete off on a fishing expedition? I was about to make an excuse to get off the phone but realized that act itself would be kind of suspicious, so I hung on the call, clenching my left fist, digging my fingernails into the palm of my hand for ten more minutes until he had to go.

"I think we're about to put in another big order," he said. I forced a smile and told him that would be great. That's all I needed to know. Did I really have to sit through "Days of our Lives" to get to it?

That's how I made it through the afternoon. Trying to appear productive. I couldn't have wanted a cigarette more.

And if Trina had been there, I most likely would have bummed one from her, but I had no idea where she was.

Until I got home. I was just through the door with take-out chicken in hand. My blonde wasn't there tonight either. (Rio, where are you?)

Instead, I went into the bathroom for a pre-dinner stroke session to the mall girl photos on my cell phone when it rang in mid-fantasy. There I was cock in hand, halfway home.

Caller I.D. told me it was Trina. I was distracted enough by the thought of cashing in my missed morning blowjob that I answered it.

"They laid me off," she sobbed. My hard-on turned into a soft-on, so I tucked it back into my underwear, sat on the toilet lid and tried to be sympathetic.

"They said my job could be done by the same department in the home office," she said once she caught her breath. "They said it appeared like I was spending too much time away from my desk. Can you believe that?"

Actually, I could.

"I have to go around and constantly pick up everybody's sales orders because nobody will drop them off to me," she said. I felt bad when I realized I'd been guilty of making her pick up mine as well. "I have to cajole the shipping department to efficiently get everything out the door on time. This is a job that requires relationships. Do you think someone in Scottsdale who's just a voice on a phone to these people is going to be able to get stuff done as efficiently?"

I had to agree with her though I hadn't seen the cost-benefit analysis of her employ that I'm sure management had taken into consideration.

She was going through the phases of grieving. Her shock had passed. She had already slid into phase two, denial.

"So I go out a couple times an hour to smoke. It's not like I don't get my job done." She broke down into heaving sobs again.

"You wanna go get drunk?" I asked. The words just spilled from my mouth like mind puke. Once they came out, it was too late to take them back. I cringed.

After a long pause. "No," she said. "I have to sit down and do some math and figure out what I'm going to do. They gave me two-months severance and I'm going to have to dip into my savings if I can't find a job in that time."

"You will," I told her, though I was just trying to make her feel better. I had no idea if she'd ever find another job for more than minimum wage.

"A couple of weeks ago, I thought I was going to get a raise too," she sighed, her voice not as excited. At this point, I was starting to lose my ability to care. Worse, I could feel that I was losing my ability to appear that I cared, which is always the most dangerous thing anyone who knows you can discover. I had spent my compassion per diem on that moron Pete in San Diego.

"I'll call you tomorrow," she told me. I was glad to get off the line before she started crying again.

I pulled my dick out to finish jerking off, but couldn't get into the right frame of mind. Every time I thought of bending one of those mall honeys over a counter at the food court I kept thinking of Trina's sobbing and it ruined it for me.

As I headed into the kitchen to eat my chicken, my phone rang again. This time, it was Eddy.

"I just got word there's a chance the Feddies might move Carl Bishop to another town. They're a bit nervous about him being a witness to a possible felony. They'd prefer he just live his life quietly."

"When would they move him?"

"I don't have that information. Could be anytime," he told me. After which he gave me Carl Bishop's address.

Dear Diary,

Today I cut the throat of someone named Carl Bishop.
But let's make this clear. Not because I wanted to.
After nightfall, I drove back up to the Valley.
I hate the Valley.

L.A. proper is full of so many nooks and crannies bursting with character. The San Fernando Valley is where taste goes to die. As I turned off the 101 onto Reseda Boulevard all I could see were rows of 1,100 square-foot, two-bedroom one-bath homes in a dazzlingly bland array of faded colors. An entire subdivision of tiny somewhat rundown postwar homes seemingly in need of a good coat of paint. Past that, it was all commercial. I noticed something today. In strip mall after endless strip mall in the Valley, there's a pattern. Each little shopping plaza on every corner seemed to have its own cigarette store or donut shop. You could tell the classy strip malls right away because they had both.

I turned off one main street onto a seemingly identical twin, then onto a third while I weaved my way out toward the little patch of this suburban hell where Carl Bishop lived.

I could have chosen a quicker route. 405 North to the 118 West but I wanted to take some time. I had to think. Only once had I not killed with purpose.

Red.

It had been a mistake. I had lost my head for just a moment and gave in to an impulse. We all take that one brief second and think, "what would it be like if I..." But maybe it was my frustration, maybe I was tired. Either way, I regret killing Red and I will continue to regret it until my dying day.

I have strayed off the path. Which is exactly why I must get back on and push harder to continue my work. To make amends for the wrong I have done.

This is why I had to kill Carl Bishop.

His was a killing of survival. Of mine. Of Eddy's.

Though he didn't say it, I could sense there something about Carl Bishop being in the way that Eddy was concerned about.

Maybe Eddy's sense of justice was offended by this rat diming his Cubano gangster pals and getting rewarded with a new life in an affluent suburb? I'd like to think his concern was because his work for me isn't over.

I have value to him. I have a requisite skill he needs. You can't just put an ad in Craigslist for a humanity janitor.

My hackles rose when I got up to the same neighborhood where I had dumped Red's body. I had a raw feeling shooting through my nerves, like short sharp shocks of electricity firing harshly from synapse to synapse in a frantic crescendo.

I continued driving through, turning down one residential street, then another, until I found a block where my parked car would blend in like any other.

It was a good mile or so walk back to where I would wait.

I climbed the rising dirt driveway up past the low-slung concrete water reclamation facility and aside from the noise of the freeway a hundred yards away, all I could hear were crickets and the crunch of my shoes on the dirt. Beyond that, I passed the construction site to the top of the hill.

From here, I could look down across the street at the exact spot where I had shoved Red from my car into the culvert.

Even with no streetlights, in the moonlight my car would have been plainly visible from here. There was no doubt in my mind.

But still no way to see my license plate from 100 feet away without binoculars or a telephoto lens. I turned and checked behind me. There was nothing here other than tall dried grass and dozens of sections of four-foot-wide concrete sewer pipe waiting to be laid. I could picture it. In two years, there'd be 20 houses here. New four-bedroom, twenty-five-hundred-square-foot, three-car-garage jobs for the modern yuppie. Rows of cookie-cutter homes with postage-stamp yards and identical mailboxes lining the street.

Conforming neighborhoods and building plans all financed with conforming loans. A little piece of America for everyone.

A truck roared past on the highway and I could hear it clear as day. Had I lived here, I could close my eyes and pretend it was the sound of waves crashing on the beach.

I could also eat dogshit and pretend it was steak.

There was little to do but wait. I walked back through the overgrown dry grass and found one of the concrete sewer pipes sitting on the ground in such a way as to give me a good view up and down the whole field. I grabbed the rebar support bisecting the opening and pulled myself inside and promptly got a face full of cobwebs when I sat down.

After brushing them out of my hair and mouth, I sat back. In my all-black sweats and cap, nobody would see me.

My breathing slowed as I listened to the traffic roar by less than a football field away. For a moment, I tried counting cars, but so many were coming and going I instantly lost track. Where were all these people headed? What were they doing? Were they happy? Sad? Drunk? Depressed?

Or did they even care at all?

I saw the glowing amber dot of his cigarette from far away. The insomniac had arrived. Possibly returning to hopefully catch a glimpse of some other illicit activity there in the shadow of the 118 Freeway overpass. I watched that glowing tip bob through the air and I was immediately struck by something. Not the desire for a cigarette but complete annoyance that here he was smoking near all of this dried grass. The joke about L.A. having four seasons is true: sunshine, mudslide, earthquake and brushfire. Some people don't think.

And that's when I heard the padding of the dog coming toward me. His dog. Off leash.

I reached into my knapsack and pulled out the rope. I had a feeling the dog would make noise, and I'd have to be quick about it.

As Carl heard his dog barking, he came closer. He didn't run away. He had no fear.

And I stepped out from behind one of the sewer pipes, grabbed him by the hair and with one sharp stroke, slashed open his jugular with a box cutter. In the dim moonlight, I could see the dark blood jetting from his neck as he went limp.

I said nothing. I wanted the rumble of traffic on the 118 to be the last thing he heard before he died.

After carefully dragging his body into one of the concrete sewer sections, I picked up the leash he had dropped, and then went back to where I had tied the dog to the rebar in the pipe that had been my hiding place. He was still happy devouring the pack of hot dogs I'd left him. I let him finish before putting the leash on him.

On the way back, I found the cigarette butt Carl Bishop had dropped. On the tip was the tiniest ember still alive, something only noticeable in the dark. I shook my head in disgust and stepped on it before walking back to my car.

FIFTEEN

Dear Diary,

I have decided to call the dog Hannah after my first grade teacher, because she too, was a bitch. So far, Hannah's been fine thanks to a supply of beef franks. She doesn't seem too torn up about her previous owner. Guessing by the looks of her, she's maybe ten, eleven years old. Judging from her behavior, I'd actually peg her as a shelter dog. Possibly picked by the late Carl Bishop to enhance the image of his new identity—a mere prop. The thought made me angry, as did the thought of someone dumping this old dog at the pound. Discarded pets that old are the first they kill at shelters to make room for animals that at least have a chance. Discarded pets that old are the ones upon which the vets in training practice their euthanasia techniques because an old dog is less likely to bite. An elderly cat won't try to claw you as you slip the catheter needle into their leg. In some shelters with limited resources, the old animals are the ones some trainees learn on, poking and prodding with needles, stabbing the suffering creatures in the heart or throat with their needles because they don't know better.

Trina has called twice today. Both of her messages sounded needy. I am starting to get a bad feeling about this.

I've been checking my phone all morning. So far no messages from Eddy. No e-mails.

He had to know about Carl Bishop. Right?

Which has made me start to wonder if it was such a good idea to stuff the body into the sewer pipe. Even though it was dark out, I could clearly recall the site.

And it hit me just a while ago like a ton of bricks what I hadn't seen.

Construction machinery.

Usually on an active site you'd see some earthmovers, a steamroller, concrete mixers. None of that stuff was there last night. No crew was going to show up and find Carl Bishop. For all I know, those concrete sewer sections may have just been dumped there as storage and will never be used.

Someone will stumble across him. Someone will see the flies.

I made a pair of omelettes. Four egg whites for me. Two, yolk and all, for Hannah. I should run out later and get some real dog food. No news on Carl Bishop. I wasn't expecting any on Bronwyn Baker. I'm sure it made a page seven somewhere, buried where nobody will see it.

Checked my e-mail again. Still nothing from Eddy. And then, all of a sudden, I remembered how I was pretty certain they were watching me and I froze. How could I have forgotten? What was going on in my head? Was I blacking out?

I sat back on the couch and pretended like I was watching some old movie on TV, but really I wasn't paying attention. I was trying to remember if there had been any stretch of time I was unable to account for. Any holes in my memory.

But then I thought if there had been, would I even realize?

How do you know if you've gone insane?

I stroked the fur around Hannah's neck and knew I couldn't keep her.

After taking her for a walk, I called Trina back. She had been crying. I thought it had been about her stupid job, but I had been wrong. She had found a lump on her cat's neck.

"I'm sure it's nothing," I reassured her. Whether or not I believed it was immaterial.

Dear Diary,

Today is day number eight without a cigarette. I can feel my lungs pinkening with every new breath. Quick breakfast of toast while I walked Hannah. Getting colder and darker now in the morning. None of my neighbors know that I have her since she's so quiet.

Found old my radio headphones in a drawer yesterday, popped in a fresh pair of batteries and to my surprise they worked. Wore them out with Hannah. Think last time I used them was years ago when I had delusions of joining a gym.

Nothing in the news but as I walked I recalled a dream I had. Two kids riding dirt bikes at the construction site found Carl Bishop's body. Made me feel like shit. Never intended for kids to see that. I remember thinking I should have known better though—that between the pair of them, there would probably be enough future psychiatrist visits to pay for a small boat. As my feet continued down the sidewalk, I had to remind myself over and over that it wasn't real. They still hadn't found him yet.

Still no word from Eddy.

Got in to the office early. Signed in. Miss Corn-fed didn't even look up from her phone. Spent all morning trying to parse the new sales reporting procedures. I thought of all the man-hours wasted trying to be more efficient. I guess if my customers get their shit and I can waste time and blame it on the system, what the fuck do I care?

Found a nearly whole newspaper in the men's room. In the obits today, Terry Walditz. Age 34. Wrote a best-selling book on the raw food diet. Died in a multiple car wreck in Hermosa Beach. So young. So full of life. So fucking what if all you eat is plants and nothing that had a mother if in the end you end up pinned under the crushed roof of your whip choking on your own blood as your legs go numb and your limbs go cold? Is it possible Terry Walditz's last living thought on this mortal plane was: "I could have had steak!"

Just shows you that you can live your life with the illusion of some kind of rule and structure and it's all swell and grand until you wake up one morning, get out of bed and step on a cosmic banana peel.

I'm sure Terry Walditz has the purest digestive tract and cleanest conscience of any dead guy in the L.A. County morgue.

I may just have to go to the funeral, but I'm definitely not staying for lunch.

Someone brought a birthday cake for some schlub who was let go yesterday, so they just put it in the break room. Whiney-Ass joked it was death cake as he cut a second piece for himself with the 8-inch knife someone had thoughtfully supplied the kitchen with. As he wiped the frosting from the blade with one of his dirty fingers, I thought of how ultimately satisfying it would be if I were to take the knife out of his hand and plunge it into his chest—the sucking sound the wound would make as his punctured lung desperately pulled air through it. The sudden gasp he would emit as I brought the blade down again, this time aiming directly for his heart, ramming the tip through the tough muscle of his ventricle would sound to my ears like a Mozart sonata. As I brought the blade up a third time, I would feel the handle effortlessly rotate in my palm to go from an overhand to underhand grip.

With an arc like a Pete Townshend windmill guitar chord, I would stab him in the crotch just above the pubis, tearing the blade upward through his abdomen so I could loose his entrails onto the ground.

Then I would run my finger along the blade to wipe off his blood before licking it clean.

And as Whiney-Ass put the knife down next to the cake box, I picked it up and held it firmly, feeling its weight in my hand as I contemplated the ultimate OSHA violation.

Then he turned to me, his lips covered with red and green frosting as I lowered the knife into the death cake and sliced a small piece for myself.

"Having some trouble there?" he asked, seeing my hand shake. "Damn thing's barely sharp enough to cut through a cake."

"Guess they're afraid the layoffs will make someone do something drastic," I joked.

"They must realize we're a gun society," he said.

"I'm surprised, given the average climate of the American office, that there aren't workplace shootings every day," I told him, quite seriously.

"Tell you what," he winked. "They let us go, I say we suit up and go all Kleebold and Harris on this place."

I put my cake down and walked out. It's one thing to kill with a purpose and another entirely to be a pair of pimply-faced dickless cowards shooting innocent people at point blank range because you finally got sick and fed up of all the wedgies.

Dinner at home was pepperoni pizza hot pockets and mostly wilted salad out of a bag. Miso dressing from Trader Joe's. Very nice. I spent two hours researching the Interstate Slasher on the Web. I made a map of where his victims had been dumped. I read every story looking for any pattern, anything so small the cops would overlook.

My cell rang. It was Trina. I almost picked it up, but let it go to voice mail instead. She asked if I was home, and I swear I could detect something in her voice. I can't quite describe it, but it really made me think she already knew I was. Honestly, I got very freaked out. My first thought was to peek out my blinds to the parking lot, but I had to remind myself to keep frosty and not let on that I knew anything was up.

I waited ten minutes, and then called her back.

And then it hit me. What if they had bugged my place? You can just as easily find those kinds of electronics online. Anybody could do it. How hard would it be to gain entry into my place at work? I had thought of adding another lock, but that kind of thing brings attention, especially by the nosy old biddies down the hall. As Trina yakked on, I nervously checked around, at the lamp that now seemed to me as if it had been moved, the electric socket that looked newer than I remembered. I cradled the phone between my shoulder and ear and got down on my hands and knees and searched among the dust bunnies for anything out of place—maybe an old cell phone wired to a long-term battery. As I stood, I saw a small spackle mark on the wall that didn't seem familiar to me at all.

She asked me what I was up to tonight. I had planned to do some research on trying to find any patterns in the Interstate Slasher case that maybe matched up with other serial murder profiles, but instead of saying so I decided to see where this conversation was going to take me—what her gambit was. Maybe I would get lucky, and she would intentionally or unintentionally reveal a card.

Instead, she asked if I wanted to get together and fuck.

I said yes. She told me to come over around midnight and to bring my libido. I mentioned to her I was in the mood for something really dirty and I could hear her voice perk up in that way older women overreact anytime they think you're telling them how horny you make them. I told her my idea for something crazy and when I described in detail what it was, I could have sworn she was fingering herself to orgasm. After hanging up, I thought about it for a moment. I looked at the spackle hole in the wall for five minutes, running my finger over its uneven surface before grabbing my keys. I had two quick stops to make.

By the time I arrived at her place, she answered the door in the flimsy negligee I told her to put on. Her pert nipples poking up from underneath the sheer fabric. She smelled of lilac powder and lily soap having just showered. Outside, the sky had opened up. I was near soaking to the bone and I closed the umbrella I had hidden behind as I crossed the street, while I eyeballed her up and down. She gazed at the bottle of champagne in my hand and grinned. Before I peeled my wet coat off, she was all over me, purring as she pushed her tongue into my ear. I partially held back her advances, mostly to savor her desire for me, but also because I didn't want to ruin anything. From my pocket came the clothesline I had just bought a half hour earlier. With this, her eyes went wide with wild yearning.

"Tie me up," she told me in a very girlish voice as she stripped naked. "And do whatever you want to me. I've been a very bad girl."

I trussed her blindfolded and spread eagle to the bedposts. Her skin turned to gooseflesh as I cinched the first line to her right ankle.

I ran a fingertip up her leg to her thigh, toying slightly with her clit before stopping and ignoring her purrs for more. Instead, I leaned down and whispered into her ear all the nasty things she wanted me to tell her that I was going to do to her.

"I'm gonna eat your pussy until you pass out and then fuck your unconscious body," I told her, emphasizing the verbs to make it sound more violent.

Then, as she lay there quivering and wet, I put on my coat and slipped out the door.

While I crossed the parking lot of her apartment complex to my car down the block, I had to smirk at the thought of her hearing that door click and knowing if I was still there. I could imagine her calling out to me, first amused, then getting slightly more and more annoyed.

I could imagine her relief as she heard me come back inside just moments later to tell her I had another surprise for her, without revealing that I had brought in a five-pound sledgehammer from the trunk of my car.

And there was part of me that wanted to take off her blindfold so she could see it coming, but instead I just opted to raise it up in both hands and bring it down as hard as I could into her face.

As I had imagined during the drive over, her skull exploded like a watermelon, spraying the bed, spraying the wall, spraying the floor and myself.

And she never moved once, not even twitched as the hammer smashed through her face and brain, driving her hair into the gore-soaked sheet. She just lay there, still as a board.

As the burst of adrenaline faded away, my heart thumped in my chest and I reached down and touched her between her legs to find she was still moist.

I looked down at what remained of Trina and whispered goodbye before untying her body from the bed and wrapping it up inside the comforter.

SIXTEEN

Dear Diary,

The Hillside Strangler was actually not one person, but two.

However, the media didn't know it at the time, they assumed only one person was committing these heinous killings back from October 1977 to February 1978. In that span, at least ten women that the police know about were attributed to the Hillside Strangler.

As is the case with most serial murderers once caught, it's never completely assured it will be truly known how many lives they took. Every so often, a set of old bones will turn up on a hiking trail, a John or Jane Doe who will spend eternity in a cardboard box awaiting anything that could help determine identity or create some kind of closure. And somewhere in a cell or already in the ground is the killer who put that body there, the person who knows the truth and will never tell, no matter how much agony the victim's family has gone through.

On the news this morning. Possibly the worst thing I've ever heard. Parents leave their ten-month-old with grandma for a week while they go off to buy a house in another state. They fly out, find something, wrap it all up in five days and come back early. After Grandma doesn't show to pick them up at the airport, they take a cab back to her place. When they get there and let themselves in, there's no sign of her, there's no sign of the baby.

Nothing.

So they're freaking out. They call the cops who show up and the first thing the officers do is check the garage. There they find Grandma lying dead, face down on the concrete floor. And inside the car, still strapped to her baby seat was little Jessica as she had been for the past three days. Her mouth was open, frozen in the last expression she had ever made before finally expiring. The coroner ruled grandma died of a massive coronary after taking the baby with her to the grocery store, most likely moments after pulling her car into the garage and getting out. She had been crossing to the other side to get baby Jessica out when whammo.

Time stamp on the receipt had placed grandma at the Stop and Shop on Monday just after ten.

And all I could think about was this little baby sitting there waiting for grandma or anyone to come, sitting and waiting and crying for two days and nights before dying of dehydration and exposure.

Who do you blame? The parents for trying to do something for the entire family to have a better life? The American auto manufacturers for making a car airtight enough to insulate a baby locked inside?

Though I suppose if the car had truly been airtight, the story would have had the same conclusion.

That's what I thought of all morning. What it must have been like to have that baby, scared, alone, hungry and wondering why all the people who loved you had now vanished.

Terry Walditz's funeral was terrible. I have attended services at these memorial chapels—a funeral factory is more like it. Hello Sir, which service have you come to attend? Oh yes, please check the board. The Seidler funeral is in the westward chapel down this hall to the right past the Sunset Chapel and the simulated indoor rose garden.

I was one of only four other men who had attended. The one who had obviously known Terry Walditz the best had been the only person to step up and offer any semblance of a eulogy. Afterwards, I had planned on ducking their stares and questions when the same bearded eulogist cornered me by the door.

He asked how I knew Terry. I told him I had met Terry at a bar. He told me Terry had been sober for ten years.

I told him it had been a long time ago. That the day after I met Terry, I decided to get sober and I never had a chance to thank him. I could see the bearded man break into tears. He said Terry really was that kind of guy. I told him I'd never forgotten Terry, and when I saw his obituary I had to come and say thank you.

He asked if I had done it.

It took me a moment before I understood and told him I felt weird thanking Terry under the circumstances—in front of everybody.

"Nonsense," he said, then put his hand on my back and escorted me to Terry Walditz's closed casket and stood next to me with his head bowed.

I muttered a few awkward sentences. I said thank you to the wooden box in front of me. I told the box how my life had changed for the better and I had only one person to thank. I choked on my own words when I heard the bearded man sobbing next to me. I pretended to be broken up and quickly told him I had to go.

Outside, I got to my car feeling like I had to gasp for air. I drove away before anyone else came out.

There is a growing numbness on my chest. One that I fear is my body dying more and more by the minute.

They say every seven years the cells on your body die off and are replaced by new ones. In effect, that means none of your body is the same at age 35 as it was at 28. That particular incarnation of you has completely died only to be replaced by a replica, by a complete doppelganger.

By my best guess, I have smoked over sixty cigarettes in the past two days. I found the first few in Trina's purse as I began combing through it. Among her possessions were a lipstick (red), eyeliner (black), one-half pack of mint gum (sugar-free) and a wallet containing fifty-one dollars in cash, some two dollars in change, and two Visa cards. One credit, one debit.

Driver's license (decent photo, no smile, organ donor sticker). Not one photograph of family, friends. Not even one of the cat. I opened her phone. Still on, but battery low. Ten numbers in her phonebook. Two are the office. Front desk and one other that seems familiar but I can't place it.

My number, thankfully, didn't qualify for a permanent spot. This tells me she didn't think of us as boyfriend/girlfriend. If they run her recent phone records, for all the calls she made to me over the past few days, they'll come up with the pre-paid cell I bought with cash.

Eddy's not the only one with fancy tricks.

Dear Diary,

Yesterday they found her, sliced from belly to anus and when I read that in the paper, I seemed titillated somehow by the word anus. I had placed her in a remote area. I had turned her head away from the parking entrance in what would be perceived by savvy profilers as my very own personal act of contrition.

The two men known as the Hillside Strangler were Kenneth Bianchi and his cousin Angelo Buono. Their first victim was a Hollywood prostitute named Yolanda Washington. Before dumping her away from where they had strangled her, they cleaned her body. She had also been viciously raped both pre and post-mortem.

Two weeks later, on Halloween morning 1977, police found the corpse of a teenage girl wrapped up in plastic. She also had been killed elsewhere, and was found with ligature marks on her neck and body.

It was just another six days before they abducted, tortured, raped and strangled a twenty-one-year-old waitress on her way home from work.

And then, another week before the same fate awaited two girls aged 12 and 14, on their way home from school. Their naked bodies were found on a trash-strewn hillside near

Dodger Stadium. They had been used and thrown away by Bianchi and Buono like beer cans.

In three more months, they would kill five more women. With quiet 20-year-old honors student Kristina Weckler, found dead on a Glendale hillside, the duo had first attempted to kill her with lethal injections of poison before returning to strangulation.

And in February of 1978, Bianchi and Buono botched their eleventh murder and called it quits. The stranglings stopped and nobody knew why. It was only after Kenneth Bianchi had been arrested in Washington State for murdering two female Western Washington University students whom he had lured to a house he was guarding.

He strangled both of them, leaving so many clues that he was arrested almost immediately afterwards. It was when the police saw his California driver's license that they had put him together with the Hillside killings.

And though there is no direct evidence, Kenneth Bianchi is suspected to have committed the Alphabet Murders back in his hometown of Rochester, New York. Between 1971 and 1973, three young girls. Carmen Colon, Wanda Walkowicz and Michelle Maenza were raped and murdered. The case was never solved.

Carmon Colon was found in Churchville.

Walda Walkowicz was found in Webster.

Michelle Maenza was found in Macedon.

In the office, nobody had heard the news until after lunchtime. I'm not exactly sure who broke the story of Trina's death, but once they did, it spread like wildfire and you could sense a feeling inside the place like someone had sucked all the air out of the building.

I waded outside into the smoking area, where I hadn't seen so many people since the day the Fossil came and the firings started. Trina was the subject on everyone's lips. The pallor on their stunned faces made me believe beyond a shadow of doubt most had never known someone who had been murdered before.

One woman talked about her cousin who had been killed by his own girlfriend. After she found out he had been cheating, she waited until he went to sleep one night and put a loaded gun to his temple and blew his brains onto the wall. She tried to claim it was suicide, but the powder burn on her own hand told the real story.

Someone asked if anybody had heard from Trina since she was let go. I shook my head. Another woman said Trina liked to keep to herself mostly.

"It's always the loners that get killed," she said. "They talk to someone they shouldn't and..." she let it hang in the air, her raised eyebrows serving as the punctuation to her sentence.

Whiney-Ass had come over to my desk to tell me they had fired The Tool. He had gotten into a shouting match with his superior and pulled his fist back to sock the guy in the face. I had to hide my grin.

"They're dropping like flies," he said and as he walked away, I watched and fantasized about putting his hand into the paper cutter in the copy room and cutting off his fingers with the sharp machete-like blade.

Kenneth Bianchi's mother had been a destitute street hooker, much like his very first victim Yolanda Washington. He had been unwanted and was given up for adoption at birth.

It had taken no later than an early afternoon press conference by no less than the Chief of Police of Los Angeles to announce that Trina Cone, the murdered woman they had found dumped in the basin near Sunland was most likely a victim of the killer known as the Interstate Slasher.

The deception had been simple. I had read and researched enough about the real Interstate Slasher to pull off his m.o. or a reasonable facsimile thereof. Inside my car I had placed a tarp across the backseat. There I laid Trina's body across it to lessen the mess as I drove to the quiet place off the road where I took her out and cut into her torso. With a sharp knife, I removed one breast and gutted her like a fish, letting her innards spill out of her body. The purification had already begun, as had rigor mortis and the gasses released from her abdomen nearly caused me to gag.

When I rolled her over, a loud, wet farting sound came from her ass.

After stripping down to my shorts and cleaning myself as well as possible with a whole box of baby wipes, I placed everything into separate trash bags. My blood-covered sweats in one. My clothes from the other night in another. The bloody tarp I rolled up with her purse (minus the $51 I found inside to help defray the cost of the pre-paid phone I had smashed with a hammer and flushed down my toilet. In the last bag was the pair of shoes I'd worn to Trina's house. They had been two sizes too large so I wasn't sorry to not have to wear them again.

All these I disposed of along the way home, in separate trashcans behind fast food joints, in shopping centers and strip malls.

So now I wait. The police took the bait as I had planned. My gambit to draw the Interstate Slasher out of hiding has gone into effect with a debt of gratitude to Miss Big Nose. I will catch him. By doing so, I will give her life meaning. I will give her fame.

She will not have died in vain.

SEVENTEEN

Dear Diary,

Woke today completely rested, even though I was up late watching news and combing the internet for activity. Did fifty sit-ups and took Hannah for a walk. She barked once when I pulled the leash out and I had to shush her. I saw that during the night she had been clawing at the door to get out. I feel bad keeping her cooped up like this. My neighbors still don't know she's here. At least they didn't before today. We'll see what happens.

Made six eggs, scrambled. Gave half to the dog. KTLA News showed sound bytes from the police chief's presser yesterday. Nothing new. Then I almost turned off the TV to get dressed when I caught the story about the body they located up in a construction site near the 118 freeway.

Carl Bishop.

Jogger found him. Not a kid. Made me feel better. The whole story took thirty seconds including the aerial footage from the news copter and then it was onto the weather.

Partly cloudy. Highs in the mid-60s.

Put on my light yellow button-down shirt and grey slacks, black shoes. I never wear this shirt. For some reason, it usually strikes me as not being a very manly color. Today though it seemed right. It seemed, dare I say it, cheery.

I checked my phone and my e-mail. No word from Eddy.

No news isn't good news. No news is no news.

Even though I want to, I'm not reaching out to Eddy unless I have to.

On the drive into the office I thought more about Carl Bishop and something hit me like a steel hammer to the head. What proof did I actually have that he had been an eyewitness to my dumping of Red's body?

None.

I had taken Eddy's word at face value. There had been no news story about eyewitnesses. There hadn't even been a mention of Red's body being found. I tried pushing it out of my head for the moment.

After a quick stop at 7-11 for cigarettes, I lit one in the car and promised I'd try to stop again.

Over and over, I kept repeating to myself that smoking is a weakness I can conquer.

It doesn't control me.

Out for an early cigarette, two secretaries were talking about another co-worker who had died a few years back. Suicide. Apparently, she tied a clothesline to a beam in her parents' garage and kicked over the chair she had been standing on. However, by the scratch marks visible on the wall next to her and the broken fingernails on her hand, the cops determined she had changed her mind at some point mid-dangle. In the end, she fought for a life she decided to throw away.

Too little, too late.

Back-to-back sales meetings with the new supervisor via conference call. Here was someone I had never met before, who had never met me, trying to tell me how to do my job. Whiney-Ass and I looked at each other like "is this guy fucking kidding me?" All I could think of is if this clown had been in the same room, I would have gouged his trachea out with my car keys.

Afterwards, Whiney-Ass said he was taking me to lunch. I asked what the occasion was. He told me it was a surprise.

He was dressed a bit nicer than usual (new blue and red striped tie, white shirt with monogram). Given his usual retread wardrobe, I should have suspected something was up.

The entire ride over to Sonny Chow's, he sang to the radio making up dirty lyrics to all the songs. It felt like I was in the car with a ten-year-old. Though his rendition of Tears For Fears' classic *Everybody Wants to Suck My Dick* was partly amusing, I finally couldn't take it anymore and asked him to stop. He got all pissy and said he didn't realize my car came with a driver's side douchebag.

We get inside Chow's and Whiney-Ass starts bitching that they've raised the price of the lunch buffet by a dollar.

"The cost of stray cat must have gone up," he said loud enough for the hostess to hear.

At our table, he waited until I got back with my plate (short ribs, steamed gyoza, lemon chicken, shrimp lo mein, shrimp toast, asparagus with brown sauce) before spilling the news.

"I'm leaving the company," he said in a voice that implied I would care. Though I wanted to break into a huge grin, I had to keep my poker face.

"I've taken a job as Regional Sales Director for Eogen," he said.

I couldn't believe it. Pharmaceuticals?

"They had some trouble in the '80s but it's a solid company. Publicly held, so there's no Fossil making decisions based upon business ideals of the 1950s."

I wanted to tell him I thought back in the '50s people actually cared about the product they were putting out. That back in the '50s people sweated bullets over doing the job right.

"I came from pharmaceutical sales originally. It's easy as drowning kittens. Jesus, man look all around you. Depression, obesity, hypertension, erectile dysfunction, high blood pressure, insomnia, arthritis, hair loss, social phobia, migraines, bone density, hormone replacement therapy, attention deficit disorder, pink eye, lupus, food allergy, high cholesterol, chronic cough, post traumatic stress disorder, diabetes, hepatitis A, hepatitis B, hepatitis C, non-Hodgkin's lymphoma, human immunodeficiency virus, birth control, yeast infections, atopic dermatitis, Crohn's disease, motion sickness, testicular tenderness," he said. "They even have a pill for something called Restless Leg Syndrome."

"You mean when your legs don't want to stay still?" I asked.

He nodded. "Back when I was a kid, my dad already had a cure for that. It was called whiskey.

"People are all fucked up today, man. We're taking more and more pills just so we can feel less and less." He was grinning now. "It's a business that will never go away and the money involved is almost criminal."

I told him I was happy for him. If it sounded hollow, it wasn't meant to.

"Come with me," he said, his voice almost pleading. "You're a great salesman. You'd make a killing."

And as he held a steely gaze on me waiting for an answer, a sales trick as old as time, I stopped thinking about his offer, but instead of what I was seeing in his eyes.

How intentional was his choice of words?

"Home office is outside Philadelphia," he told me, finally breaking. "You'd get to travel a lot. You're single, no family, and no ties. With the kind of expense account you'd have, a guy could have a lot of fun on the road if he wanted to."

I told him to hold that thought and got up to go to the can. Inside a stall, I sat and contemplated my options.

When I got back, he wound up for another pitch. "Who knows what the future holds back at our office? I'm tired of having the job security of a Belfast valet parking attendant."

I told him I'd marinate with it and get back to him, and then I let him pick up the check.

The windows had been left up, so in the car he wrinkled his nose and commented on the smell. I told him I had accidentally left some groceries in the back seat and they spoiled. Milk, eggs, meat.

He pointed to the cardboard pine tree hanging from my rear-view mirror.

"It's gonna take more than that to get rid of this stink."

Before I could answer, he changed the subject.

"So that woman who was killed, the one with the schnoz," he said, drawing his cupped hand away from the front of his face to mimic Trina's big nose. "You ever hit that?"

I had anticipated the question all day. "No," I replied, pausing just enough to not seem like a rushed answer. "You?"

Whiney-Ass laughed. "Nope." His tone changed. "That's pretty fucked up what happened to her."

I grunted my agreement while pretending I was paying attention to the left turn I was about to make.

"All I know is that there's some crazy motherfucker out there who could benefit from one of Eogen's fine line of anti-psychotic medications."

"You should go find the guy," I said. Though it sounded natural, I was trying to make a joke that wasn't even funny without letting my brain process it first. But sometimes your mind works on instinct in ways you can't even conceive and should never question.

"Maybe I already have," he said, and I couldn't help but jam on the brakes whipping both of us forward as I came to a screeching halt in the middle of the intersection.

As I realized what I had done, that he had been joking, I hit the gas.

"There, I tried to strangle you with the seatbelt." I told him while forcing a laugh to come from my throat.

"You're a dick," he said, letting out a small chuckle and shaking his head. "You'll fit in just fine at Eogen."

I got back to find a cryptic phone message from Paul in San Diego to call him back on his cell. He answered on the second ring. He told me his soon-to-be-ex-wife called the cops on him after they'd gotten into a physical altercation.

"She started it," he said. "I finished it."

I didn't really know how to respond. My level of comfort with the conversation was below zero.

"They're putting me on unpaid leave at work," he said. "I just wanted to give you a heads up that I don't think we're gonna put in that big order I told you about."

"But you're okay?" I asked. Not because I cared, but because I was angling for a way off the phone as quickly as possible without having either of us feel the need to call the other back.

He grunted an answer I wasn't paying attention to. "If things get bad, I might have to come up there and crash on your couch," he said, and all I could think of was that I barely knew this guy.

"Ah, you'd hate that, I live in a studio apartment," I lied.

"Oh, that's how it is," he grumbled. What was that I could hear in his voice? Disappointment? Annoyance? One lunch and a few laughs and he thinks he can act like my lifelong pal?

"Well maybe you shouldn't hit your fucking wife," I told him and hung up, realizing the words had come a bit loudly given the brief moment of silence in the office following my outburst.

As I went to the break room (to find another half a birthday cake for someone else I didn't know), I grabbed a root beer from the soda machine. I thought of the time I'd given Trina the Diet Coke I'd bought by accident. Before I knew it, I had my wallet out. I put a buck in the machine, bought a Diet Coke and left it on the counter.

I checked my cell phone. No messages.

The image played back in my head of standing on that hill where Eddy told me Carl Bishop had seen me dump Red. I imagined him standing there smoking his cigarette, just at the moment I had pulled up, pushed open the passenger door and rolled her down the hill.

All I could think about was that the passenger door was facing away from him. What could he have actually seen?

And what were the odds that the one eyewitness to my crime was also being hidden away by the Feds?

A thousand to one? A million to one?

The office felt warmer to me, like an oven. After going back to my desk for my sunglasses, I headed toward the front desk to sign out.

On the way, I bumped into Whiney-Ass.

"You don't look so good," he said. "Don't tell me you got a bad eggroll, because I ate two of those things."

I pushed past him.

"Don't forget what we talked about," he quietly called after me.

As I picked up the clipboard and logged a phony sales call as my excuse to get out of there, Miss Corn-fed kept staring at me.

"What?" I barked, not meaning to be so sharp with my tone. She recoiled from my voice and her perma-smile vanished momentarily. For that moment, I could see her real self. Under that makeup and pretty grin, she was lonely and sad. Most likely older than I had first thought. Probably divorced from her high-school sweetheart, out here in L.A. off the bus from Kansas to try and follow some hollow dream of getting into pictures. A dream that will never happen, even for someone as pretty as her, and she knew it.

Timidly, she pointed to my shirt. I looked down to see the root beer I must have spilled on myself without noticing.

"Yeah, I just got it cleaned," I told her, feigning my annoyance having been caused by something as trivial as that. "Sorry... for shouting."

Her phony grin came back. "It's okay. I'm having one of those days, too."

What? I almost asked. You didn't get a callback for that toothpaste commercial because the casting director thought you were too old?

Instead, I turned and left without returning the smile. I had bigger problems to deal with.

And again, I fought the traffic all the way up to the Valley, getting stuck in the glacier-like pace of the parking lot known as the 405 freeway. In the car, I found half a Snapple Mango Madness from a couple days ago.

It took me almost two hours to get up to the 118. I headed west. The sun was setting fast and I knew there wouldn't be much daylight left.

Again I parked my car far away. In the trunk were some sweats and sneakers that I changed into to look more like a jogger.

As I pretended to run, I realized I was getting winded faster than I would have thought. My knees started to ache.

When I got to hill above the culvert, I waited until no cars were passing to go down for a look. The concrete ditch had overgrown with weeds. I checked my position relative to where I thought I had pulled the car over that night.

And as I walked up the culvert, pushing the weeds away I saw it.

Her foot.

EIGHTEEN

Dear Diary,

Fuck. I cannot sleep. Every time I close my eyes, it flashes in my mind like Hiroshima. When I saw Red still lying there in the culvert exactly where I had dumped her, the feeling was like being gut punched. I doubled over and threw up onto the ground.

After wiping my mouth with the back of my hand, I forced myself to look. I pushed the weeds away to see her torn green dress covering her purple and bloated skin—the thick blanket of wriggling white maggots completely covering her face and crawling through her red hair.

It is not her death or dead body that caused me to be ill, rather the realization of the truth. The cops never found her.

Eddy has been lying to me. He's been using me.

I have been playing possum, lying in bed, keeping my eyes closed, pretending to sleep in case they are watching. I was careful driving out there yesterday, watching for a tail. I was careful when I got out and walked to the culvert. Nobody saw me.

At least, I'm pretty sure nobody saw me.

Nobody ever sees me. Of my own choosing I walk through this world like a ghost in order to disappear between the cracks. The real me remains subverted at all times. I am only alive during the moments I am doing my work. Aside from that, I blend in, I am nothing. I am vapor.

Over and over I have checked my phone, willing it to ring. If they are waiting for me to make the next move, they are sadly mistaken.

Dear Diary,

Called in sick to the office when I realized I had been staring at the screen of my computer past nine a.m. searching for news. Phil Testaleone, Tito Gomez, Bronwyn Baker, Carl Bishop.

Sam and Arthur Tancredo.

The brothers had been reported missing by their parents after not coming home that night. The two boys had been in trouble with the law before, so it was no surprise the cops treated it like the pair had run away. Kids hoof it all the time.

Their parents never believed it. Only one of their bikes had been missing. How far could they have run away riding tandem on a single 3-speed?

At school, they gathered all the grades into the auditorium and a policeman came to ask if anybody knew anything, if anybody had seen anything. Had he asked if anybody smelled anything, I might have raised my hand to tell him of the scent not unlike a backyard barbecue coming from their roasting flesh inside the shed.

We were asked to keep our eyes open. Teachers passed out flyers and we went around town, masking tape in hand, hanging them in shop windows, on street corners and telephone poles. A rumor had gone around that there was a kid snatcher terrorizing the area—some crazy guy living in his car, though it wasn't true. Parents started keeping their little ones inside under curfew.

I kept thinking about the pained look on the face of the cop who had come to our school assembly. He hadn't asked for this. The Tancredos, by virtue of their behavior, were causing the whole town to be miserable. At first, I hated them even more until I realized I was the only one with the power to make it all stop. That night, using my non-writing hand, I scribbled a note telling the cops where to look and mailed it in the morning.

Two days later, they went to the old train yard, even though they claimed they had searched there once. Inside what remained of the burnt-out shell I had described, they discovered the two charred skeletons.

What I heard later was they had found the two brothers huddled in the corner, clutching each other, burnt skulls twisted in agony.

And within a few days, the world inside my neighborhood returned to normal. Curfews were lifted; people went back to their lives able now to focus on their own quiet desperation instead of the desperation of others.

Took Hannah for a walk later than usual. One of the old biddies a couple of doors down saw me and stared, her steely eyes registering the furry interloper by my side. I usually smile at my neighbors. Today, I drained the emotion from my expression, hoping she would read that as my indifference to what I may have to do to her face with a wrench or pipe if she were to cause me any trouble. Without acknowledging anything, she went back inside her apartment and I could hear the deadbolt click behind me.

Dogs can sense things we can't, and Hannah is no exception. She had been very agitated this morning, barking incessantly at a picket fence. I turned my head, almost able to hear another dog stalking back and forth on the other side, but Hannah's noisy protestations blocked everything else out. At the corner, she barked at a Mexican kid on a bicycle causing him to almost crash while trying to steer around us. I invite him to give me that same dirty look again when I have my backpack with me.

When we returned, I was ready. I had been on the fence until the final couple of blocks. I checked my printer to make sure it had paper before opening up Word to type a letter to the police.

Dear Diary,

When Edmund Kemper III was a ten-year-old boy growing up in Santa Cruz, California, he would sneak out of his house at night to go peeping through the windows of his teacher's house and watch her undress, while fantasizing about killing her and having sex with her corpse.

One day, at the tender age of fifteen, he blew away both of his grandparents. The murder weapon had been a rifle that had been taken away from him after he was discovered using it to kill neighborhood pets. Later, when questioned by police, Edmund Kemper III told them he did it because he wanted to know what it would be like to shoot grandma to death. He was imprisoned in a mental facility and let go five years later when he was determined by his doctors to no longer be a threat to society.

Today I mailed one copy of the letter to the LAPD Headquarters downtown, the other to the L.A. Times. I wore rubber gloves as I took the printouts and folded them inside their envelopes. I wore rubber gloves as I drove several miles until I found a mailbox by the curb of a post office.

Now I'm back home, staring at my telephone, knowing I did the right thing.

Now, I wait.

Dear Diary,

I fell asleep at my desk, my face down in the newspaper; drool coming from the sides of my mouth onto my chin, when my cell rang.

"You're making a mistake," came the voice.

I was still in a haze. I'm fairly certain all I said was "What?"

"You're making a big, big mistake. It's not too late to take it back," the voice said.

And that's when I finally recognized Whiney-Ass' dulcet tone.

"How come you didn't tell me you put in a transfer to the home office a week ago?"

"Huh?"

He repeated the question. I squeezed the bridge of my nose. I had zero recollection of anything to that effect, and I told him so.

"Don't treat me like an idiot. This chick I'm friendly with in H.R. told me when I mentioned that I was raiding the place for warm bodies to take with me."

"You're nailing a chick from H.R.?" I asked.

"No, they'd make me fill out a form. What a load of crap." He sighed. "When was I going to find out? When I got a postcard from Scottsdale?"

"Yeah, maybe."

"You're such a dick. I'm telling you. You'll be miserable cooped up there with all the rules and paperwork. You'll never see the light of day. Come with me."

I told him I'd think about it. Otherwise I'd never get him off the line. Even if the job was better, the company better, the money better, I'd still have Whiney-Ass as my supervisor. It was a proposal as attractive as being asked to jump out of a moving car.

Honestly, I'd rather shit out a ball of fishhooks.

Hannah stared up from the floor and looked away from me like I wasn't even there. I realized she was too old to get attached to me this easily. I was just food and shelter to her. She knew how to play the game.

I checked my phone again. I checked my e-mail again.

And it occurred to me that maybe by not calling Eddy, I was doing something suspicious. My mind went in circles until I squeezed my eyes shut and forced it to stop.

I had to get out of my place. As I sat at my desk, I could suddenly see things I hadn't noticed before: cracks in the ceiling, walls that needed painting, carpet that needed cleaning. I had been so self-absorbed that this was the first time these things had even registered in my mind.

Dust bunnies under the couch. Cobwebs in the corners.

Funny how it's right there in front of your face and your brain just refuses to acknowledge it until one day when the curtain is pulled away.

Expired milk in the fridge. Dirt under my nails.

My place was beginning to feel like a dump. I was aware of the mess. I was aware of the smell. I had to get out. After grabbing Hannah's leash, I decided on some fresh air to clear my head. I'd been buried up to my eyes in my work and putting off the inevitable. It was obvious there were definitely some decisions to make.

We got in the car and Hannah spent the whole ride with her head out of the window as we drove out to a park up in the Santa Monica Mountains. As we got closer, I could sense Hannah getting excited. All we had done was walk around my neighborhood, padding along the concrete trails of sidewalk after sidewalk. Here she could run on grass and she knew it, almost bowling me over as I opened the passenger side door for her to get out.

I grabbed my paper and sat at a bench with a good view of the park and watched Hannah dash fifty yards to a large oak tree to take care of her business, then dash off, tail wagging to beat the band.

Hiding behind the news as I pretended to read it, I thought about Whiney-Ass' phone call. Though he and I shared lunch a couple times a week, I have always viewed it as a work friendship, nothing more. We never spoke about hanging out on the weekends or getting a poker game together. I mostly took him up on his offers to go out to eat because he had his finger on the pulse of the company and anything worth knowing; he was nosy enough to find out. He was my early warning system—an alarm that made a braying, annoying sound with each stupid comment.

As I thought about the things he's said to me—about what little he actually knows about me, something didn't add up.

If I was pretending to be his friend, why shouldn't I think he was pretending to be mine? Why am I so special to think he didn't have some kind of agenda involving me?

In 1972, Edmund Kemper III struck again at the age of twenty-four. After picking up two hitchhiking college girls, he drove them to a remote area, then put one in the trunk while he first killed the other in the back seat with a knife. He then stabbed the second one to death, later remarking how surprised he'd been at how many blows it took to end her life. He then drove both of them back to his apartment where he dissected their corpses and cut off their heads. There he kept them for days before toting their bodies out in garbage bags and burying their arms and heads in separate locations.

On September 15th, exactly one day after killing a fifteen-year-old hitchhiker and raping her dead body, Edmund visited his two court-appointed shrinks who both declared him completely sane, while at the same time asking the court to expunge his juvenile record.

Edmund Kemper III would go on to murder four more women, ending his spree by beheading his domineering mother, then repeatedly raping her headless corpse.

Afterwards, he left a note for the police and fled, turning himself in a few days later. When asked, he told the cops he was burnt out.

I put the paper down and realized two hours had passed since Hannah ran off into the woods. I stood there holding her leash, calling her repeatedly before realizing that she probably didn't know her new name. I could have easily just been yelling the word "Firetruck" or "Juicebox".

I shook my head and went into the woods, taking the well-worn trail up the hill, still calling out her name hoping she'd at least recognize the sound of my voice. After a half hour, I started to think she really had run off or that someone else had grabbed her. My mind flashed to stories I had read online about people who snatched pets from dog parks or back yards for the purposes of vivisection or just to take home and torture. I thought of Hannah, trusting old dog that she was, wagging her tail as someone put her in their car and drove away, much like I had done.

I continued deeper into the woods, calling out for Hannah. Veering off the path into the denser growth, I thought of her being old. They say animals can sense the end and will go off to be alone. I thought of her maybe just curling up under a nice tree to die.

I kept looking for her until the sun started to set, and then went home.

Godspeed, Hannah, wherever you are.

In the car, I began to wonder if this was a sign of some kind—that it was time for things to change.

NINETEEN

Dear Diary,
    They printed my letter! Right there on the front page!

Dear Editor,
    You've written about me. You know of me, but you don't KNOW me. I am the man you have decided to call The Interstate Slasher. You write speculative articles about my murders, but never have you tried to analyze why I commit them, why I have been driven to do these things. When I was young, I was abused but nobody cared. My mother was a domineering bitch who never gave me the time of day unless it was attached to the back of her hand. She was a drunk and she beat me because we were poor. She beat me because she was mad at the world and the faceless man who raped her and knocked her up with me. One time, I told her I was hungry and she hit me so hard with a chair I was unconscious for three days. Even as a teenager, she hounded me and called me stupid for failing in school. At night, she would try to make it up to me in her bed, and even then, if I didn't please her, she would hit me. So do not presume to think you know me. You only know my work and you will get to know it better very soon. I have begun to kill men as well.
    Sincerely,
    The Interstate Slasher

I have to laugh. Every single bit of it made up from a phony profile I created. As the FBI discovered in a study, most serial killers have traumatic childhoods and were never able to negotiate the maturation of the masculine psyche by breaking free of their mothers.

Strangely enough, the same study found that a good number of serial killers also suffered some kind of serious head injury during childhood.

Adding the incest was just the cherry on top. So to speak.

To make the newspaper believe it was authentic, I included a second letter with details about the deaths of Phil Testaleone, Tito Gomez, Bronwyn Baker, Red and Carl Bishop that only the killer would know, including where to find Red's body.

Now, it's just a matter of time before the police add those to the list of murders the Interstate Slasher is wanted for. I have to say, if this doesn't draw out the real Interstate Slasher, then I don't know what will.

Dear Diary,

The story is all over the news today. Channel 5 did a whole piece on the history of the Interstate Slasher (too much time spent on flashy graphics and not enough getting many of the actual case facts right). Mostly they are talking about how the Interstate Slasher is making contact with the police and the press for the first time. On CNN, a talking head from the FBI was on camera spouting on about how in the past other serial killers have sent letters to taunt the authorities. Jack the Ripper, Zodiac and the BTK Killer (which to me sounds more like something you order from a drive-thru window). The talking head also spent time claiming this type of communiqué was generally a cry for help.

Usually, the Fibbies they get on camera are spokesmen, not actual agents—guys who spend their days talking to reporters and looking good on TV while the real Feds do all the legwork.

I have decided to quit smoking again to celebrate.

Besides, I need to get back into shape.

Again, I promise that if I can get this guy, I will retire. I will feel that the sacrifices that were made to eliminate this lowlife piece of shit were well worth it.

Now I wait. I can only imagine this guy watching all this coverage, seething. Here was someone else taking credit for his work. Given how well-thought-out his killings were, small details obviously planned in advance, there was a pride to what he was doing that would burn with each mention of the recent killings credited to him.

And the only two people who knew the truth were he and I. It was like electricity, the feeling of a connection between us. I was inside his head and he would know that. He would have to kill again and somehow let people know the difference between his work and that of the impostor. Maybe he'd do it in haste and somehow screw up.

I'm closer to him than ever now.

I decided to call in to work again. Burn another sick day. I stayed in and watched all the coverage and surfed the web for news. Drudge Report put it as their headline sometime after 11 a.m. I had to laugh. Everybody was buying my lie.

Quick lunch (Progresso Lentil soup from a can) during which I couldn't help but stare over at the red and white blanket in the corner where Hannah had slept. I picked it up and it smelled like dog so I decided to take it down to the laundry room and wash it. There was a twinge. I was sad for a moment and thought about driving out to look for her again, but even as I grabbed my keys I decided it would be best to put Hannah behind me.

Jack the Ripper's first victim was found at four in the morning on August 31, 1888, on a deserted street in London's seedy East End. A market porter discovered a bundle wrapped in a canvas tarp that, upon inspection, turned out to be the butchered corpse of a forty-two-year-old prostitute named Mary Anne Nichols. Her throat had been cut, her abdomen slashed and her vagina mutilated with the same knife.

What no one would realize until later is that very night, the era of the modern sex-murder would be born.

One week later, only a half mile away, the body of another prostitute, this time forty-seven-year-old Annie Chapman would turn up disemboweled, nearly decapitated and with a wound showing that the killer had partially sawed through her spine.

Afterwards, I drove over to the car wash and used nearly a whole container of bleach cleaner on my back seat where Trina's body had bled and I emptied a mostly full bottle of Febreze onto the carpets. I can't tell if the smell is finally gone, or my nose is just fucked up from so much smoking lately. It's not like I can ask anyone, unless I kill him or her afterwards if they tell me yes.

I was feeling okay, renewed in a way, knowing how much I was influencing the process, until the phone rang.

The words stunned me to the point where I had to ask for them to be repeated.

"I know you wrote that letter," Whiney-Ass told me.

I knew what he meant. "What are you talking about?" I asked.

"Don't play dumb with me. The letter. The one in the paper. I know you wrote it." He was laughing.

I don't know how long I was silent. After a moment, all I could hear was the blood rushing through my ears. Suddenly, when it rang again, I snapped to.

"I was just fucking around. You didn't have to hang up on me," he said.

"It's not funny," I replied.

"Dude, you're gonna have to learn how to take a joke if you're gonna work for me."

"Yeah, we have to talk about that." I sucked in a breath. "What are you doing later?"

Dear Diary,

You cannot tell me that what happened could have been avoided. You cannot try, because I know that once a path is chosen one must continue until they reach the end, no matter what hardships are along the way.

That night, Whiney-Ass gave me his address, but I complained that it was too far away. Instead, I gave him the name of a bar I had actually never been to. At eight o'clock, five minutes after I was supposed to hook up with him, I called to tell him my car had broken down. He offered to come over to where I was but I told him Triple-A was on their way. I let him hear the exasperation in my voice, really milking it to the point where I sounded like someone you wouldn't want to be around at that moment. I told him I'd talk to him the next day.

He had no idea that I was actually calling from inside of his house.

I waited for the next call, one that never came—the one I thought he'd make to his girlfriend, Katherine, telling her he was coming right home. If he had made it, I can just imagine the look on her face, the one that wordlessly asks 'who farted'? It had been the same look she had given me when I rang the doorbell in my Edison Uniform this late, the same look she had given my wallet when I flashed my old gym membership instead of any real credentials. But it wasn't the look she gave as I shoved her down onto the floor of her entranceway and kicked her in the stomach as hard as I could to knock the wind out of her. Even before she started crying as I tied her to a dining room chair, I could tell she was a bitch. (Girls with big fake tits usually are). Whiney-Ass never mentioned he even had a girlfriend. (Who doesn't mention at least once or twice that they have a girlfriend unless she's a total horror?) Besides, what decent chick would live with a guy like him? He's one of the most painful people on this earth. He's one of those guys that half the time just listening to him drone on and on is about as much fun as having soap in your eye.

I needed to get her talking, but I needed her under control so I dominated her fully with the back of my hand to her face several times. Over and over, I hit her again, telling her to shut up until I knew she understood by holding back her whimper.

Mentacide.

I told her I was going to ask her some questions and if I wasn't satisfied with the answers I was going to cut into her. I even slashed the palm of her hand with the box cutter to make it clear as a mountain stream how serious I was. As I snapped off a fresh blade, I began my little interrogation.

In the end, it was messy, but it worked—she told me everything I needed to know.

And I barely let her suffer. If at all, it was because of how she spit on me the moment she realized I was going to have to kill her. I clamped the plastic bag over her head quick as a wink, but in retrospect, there was no need to stab her eyes out and I didn't have to hover her face, grinning as she pulled for air that would never come.

Besides, the bag wasn't see-through anyway. She had no idea what I was doing.

I also regret feeling her up afterwards.

But how could I pass it up? Her fake ones were spectacular. I lifted her shirt and gave each one a squeeze, but it didn't feel right with the glove on. They were harder than I expected them to be. Maybe too big for her frame.

So I untied her from the chair, laid her on the floor and sliced out her implants with the box cutter. The first one, I screwed up and carved through the stiff polymer bag as the blade punched through the skin of her left breast, spilling gooey clear gel everywhere.

Which is why I was a bit more careful removing the right one. I followed the plastic surgeon's initial incision under the breast, slicing through the epidermis and dermis until I had cut almost the whole way around. I lifted the skin up and there it was, a transparent, bloodstained bag of silicone. I picked it up in my hand and even in the low light I could see it was stamped with "500cc" and EoGen Pharmaceutical's name.

I wonder if Whiney-Ass got them wholesale.

Now that I think about it, I'm fairly certain it's entirely possible the size of the implant is inversely proportional to the amount of self-esteem.

She looked like a bitch that needed them in order to get guys to like her. I had a feeling she was a really terrible person and if it hadn't been me, then it would have just been somebody else.

I think I can believe why Whiney-Ass didn't call her when he found out he was going to be free for the evening. Either he had something on the side or he was happy to sit anywhere but next to this horror show all night long and probably have a few drinks to boot.

In fact, I believe he'll even come home with the intention of telling her that I did show up and he helped talk some sense into me and that he was glad to help and all that happy crappy bullshit.

And when he does come through that door, Whiney-Ass is in for one hell of a surprise when he steps out of his perfectly furnished entranceway and looks down at what's in the chair I carefully dragged over.

After I grab him and incapacitate him too, I'm going to get the truth out of him if I have to slice it away inch by bloody inch.

Because I know he knows Eddy.

She told me so. With one of her last breaths, she told me so.

And now we sit and wait for him to show up. One drink, two drinks.

We sit and wait. I don't care if it's all night.

TWENTY

Dear Diary,

I opened my eyes and it took me a minute to remember where I was. I hadn't made mental note of it before but Whiney-Ass' house was much nicer than I thought it would be.

Honestly, I wasn't really sure what to expect. Instead of Ethan Allen and flowers, perhaps a giant watercolor over the fireplace of Jesus having sex with underage boys or something?

I was wrong. What do I know?

This is how it all happened to the best of my memory.

I heard Whiney-Ass' car pull up about quarter to one. There was the soft thud of the door slamming and his moderately intoxicated key fumbling for several seconds before he stumbled inside.

"Sorry, I'm late!" he announced with the hint of a slur. "Guy's such a fucking zero, I don't know why I asked him to come work with me," he mumbled as slid off his jacket.

It was only a matter of seconds, possibly less than two, though it seemed like time had frozen entirely, before he stopped talking and the sobbing began.

And as I stepped out from inside the hall closet, there he stood, jaw agape, staring at Katherine slumped over, tied back to the dining room chair, her torso bloody and sliced to ribbons.

When he finally heard my footsteps behind him and turned, it was too late. My stun gun caught him above the left pectoral muscle and I shot fifty thousand volts into his body to knock him to his knees. His body wavered, almost collapsing to the floor, but a handful of his hair kept him upright until the device recharged and I could give him another shock right to his neck below his chin.

As I stood there in his quiet house, alone except for his unconscious body on the floor, it brought me back to a place I wasn't at all comfortable with.

I guess if you want to be crude about it he'd been fucking her for two months. That's all it was, I saw the way he looked at her. I may have been young, but I knew what that cold stare meant. She was nothing to him other than a piece of ass.

I'll never forget that moment she broke my heart, pulling me aside into my room, sitting me on the edge of my bed while she knelt before me. I was 14. I can remember it as clear as a spring day. She had on her beige cotton dress with the red floral pattern. It had been her favorite even back before dad died.

Her words cut into me, and I could feel them slicing up my insides as my mind exploded from the sheer anguish of what it all meant.

"You can't marry him," I pleaded. I had always kept my mouth shut about Jerry the same as I had about the other half dozen or so men who she had brought home for any extended period of time. He had a good job as a truck dispatcher and he kept her warm on cold nights. Those were his qualifications.

"He's abusive," I mumbled numbly. He had never struck her or even raised a hand to me but I could see it in his glare, like that of a predator.

It didn't even sting when she slapped me across the face. I had already been crying.

That night, Jerry came over for dinner, smelling of cheap beer. Mom had picked up a six-pack for him on the way home and right after dinner, he sat with me on the couch, cracking open another can as he fumbled all over the words telling me that he was going to be my new dad now and how he and my mom would probably have a few more kids.

Inside that look of his, I could see the desire to be my friend was about as great as my desire to pour acid into my eyeballs.

After he finished his lengthy speech, repeating the same things five or six times, I showed him how grateful I was by taking his empty beer and bringing him a fresh one from the refrigerator.

That night, in bed, my eyes burned with tears. I didn't recognize the woman who had tucked me in. She was tired and ugly and I was a responsibility that seemed to hinder her pursuit of some kind of stability. I stared at the electric alarm clock by my bedside, counting second-hand sweeps until well after midnight before going into the kitchen to get a knife.

"I now understand why spanking a child is a good thing," I told Whiney-Ass as he came to while I was throwing the third plastic mixing bowl full of ice water into his face. "A child who endures his first spanking will suddenly understand what it's like to be hurt to the point of tears. The impression it makes hopefully keeps that child from later doing something stupid, something that will either get them punished again or otherwise result in feeling that level of physical pain. A child who has been spanked realizes there are consequences to his or her actions."

I looked right into his eyes.

"You were never spanked, were you?"

His head shook side to side slightly as if he were experiencing some kind of tremor.

He'd been tied to the chair using a clothesline I'd found in the laundry room and I had wedged a sock from his dresser into his mouth, primarily to keep him from screaming, but also to keep him from possibly spitting blood on me. Honestly, after all the fucked-up drunk girls he's bragged about banging I didn't want to risk getting A.I.D.S from his bodily fluids.

"I also found this." I held up the latex double dong he had barely hidden next to his underwear. "You might want to wash this thing every now and then. There's a crusty layer of God knows what on there."

He mumbled something, screamed it really, though his voice was completely muffled. I believe it was "fuck you".

Grabbing him by the hair with one hand, I braced my other arm on his shoulder and let out a loud grunt as I yanked out a small handful of his thinning dye-jobbed mane by the roots.

The patch of scalp was barely the diameter of a golf ball but I could see it bleeding.

I tossed it aside and leaned into his ear. "How do you know Eddy?" I growled now that I was pretty sure I had proved to him how serious I was. I showed him the blade I used on Katherine and let him know I'd cut him slow if he screamed before taking the sock out of his mouth.

"We're related," he spat out, barely able to speak. I had to pull back to keep from getting sprayed with blood and mucous. What he said next, I couldn't quite make out because all of a sudden, it felt as if the floor had fallen out from under my feet.

I could hear her sleeping as I stepped lightly into her bedroom and brought the serrated knife down into her throat, tearing the blade quickly across her neck so she wouldn't suffer.

Jerry had passed out on the sofa in front of the TV, as was his normal routine. A bomb could have gone off and not woken him up so it was easy for me to pick up the large ceramic lamp off the end table and smash it over his big stupid head. The plan I had made, laying there, scheming away, was to make it look like a burglary gone bad.

The sound of the breaking porcelain was very satisfying, like a cold spoonful of ice cream on a hot day. Jerry tumbled off the couch onto the floor and, because he wasn't much bigger than I was, it wasn't that hard to drag him into the kitchen.

There on the top of his melon, I could see the large knot coming up; swelling to the size of a ripe plum under the flap of skin my blow had torn away. As I got him inside the kitchen, I turned on the light and began rummaging through the utensil drawer until I found the meat tenderizer. I looked at the square head of the steel hammer, covered in row after row of tiny pyramid shaped points and I whacked that lump onto Jerry's head once, then twice hoping to crack his skull open to no avail. Finally, I turned the meat tenderizer to the flat side and used it to pound a steak knife into the bone of his skull right in the middle of his forehead until it stuck.

Which is exactly when Jerry came to. The fear I felt when his eyes popped open was like an icy claw wrapping its sharp talons over my balls. With a sound like some kind of feral animal, he managed to shove me backwards hard enough that I smashed the back of my head on the edge of the counter top. The meat tenderizer slipped from my hands and Jerry picked it up and threw it at me, hitting me square in the face, breaking my nose.

And somehow, he managed to get up onto his feet, staggering toward me with that same predatory look in his eyes that I had seen countless times before. I could see salvation in the form of the kitchen door and I tried to turn and run but my head felt as if two explosions had hit it, one from behind and one from in front. My vision had gone blurry and my legs felt like rubber. I would later realize the blow against the counter had given me a concussion.

Jerry wrapped his big, thick hands around my neck, mumbling something I couldn't make out and I weakly tried to push him away as his grip tightened. My throat felt as if I had a cinder stuck deep in it as he started choking the life out of me. Finally, I was able to bring my knee up into his crotch and I pulled away. Then as he doubled over, I grabbed a skillet off the stovetop and smashed it down hard against Jerry's back.

I can still remember the crunching sound when he hit the floor face first hard enough to drive the knife the rest of the way into his skull.

There I collapsed, onto the floor, waiting to see if he was still alive—hoping he wasn't because I was in no shape to fight anymore. After a few minutes, I reached my hand up into the utensil drawer and came out with another knife. It took all of my inner strength to cut into my face, my hands and to finally stick the blade three inches into my stomach.

There had been more blood than I thought and I knew I had to act quickly, so I put the knife in Jerry's dead hand before crawling with all my might to get to the phone and dial the operator for help.

As I lay in the hospital, I told the police detectives that Jerry had lost his temper after my mom told him he had to leave because she wasn't going to marry him. I told them he had been drinking, that he killed her and he and I struggled in the living room and kitchen after he tried to kill me. A fair amount of alcohol found in his blood backed up my story.

In the two weeks I remained in that bed, recuperating from my wounds, I realized my only regret was that I had made a mistake in trying to kill Jerry in the kitchen. Too many weapons of opportunity.

Live and learn.

I don't know how long I was out, but I came to as I was laying flat on the floor in Whiney-Ass' house. My jaw felt like it had been struck with a brick and I looked up to find Whiney-Ass struggling to wriggle free of the last coils of rope holding him to the chair.

He had used his legs to lift himself up and drive the top of his head into my chin.

All I recall is seeing stars and my vision going blurry and the pitch of his voice rising like a steam kettle while he lay there on his side struggling to get out of the rope. What happened next, happened not because of anything other than pure instinct. Before he could make another sound, I leapt upon him, clamping my one hand over his mouth as I pinned his left arm behind him with my other. "Do what I tell you or I'll hurt you worse than you could even imagine," I growled in no uncertain terms. I nodded toward Katherine, still strapped to her chair nearby.

He didn't need to be told twice.

I kept his arm pinned behind his back as I picked up his wet sweat sock from the floor and stuffed it back into his mouth, shoving deep with two of my fingers until I heard him gag on the wad of cotton. He was going to need it. As I helped him up, I yanked his forearm up toward his shoulder blade, snapping the humerus with a loud wet crack.

I held his shaking body and let him cry out his muffled scream.

My head was still underwater from the blow he'd laid on my chin. I barely had the strength in my knees to hold myself up, let alone the two of us. I tied him back to the chair, this time going for my backpack to get what was left of the duct tape so I could wind great long strands around his wrists and ankles holding him in place. He wasn't going anywhere. There, on the floor where I'd dropped it, I found my stun gun and something inviting about the green glowing indicator telling me it was charged made me zap Whiney-Ass' stupid whiney ass until he passed out.

I was feeling it as well. My mind was screaming at me to lie down. I hadn't slept in twenty hours and the space between my ears was ringing like a fucking cathedral.

But no, I suddenly realized that wasn't what I heard ringing.

I snatched my phone from my pants pocket and I suddenly felt a sense of dread as it stopped, because, for just that moment, I wasn't quite sure what I had heard. My head felt like a rubber hot water bottle full of baseballs and I knew I had to sit.

And I knew, because I could hear my ninth grade gym teacher's voice in my head, I mustn't sleep. I was at least still sharp enough to know that if I have a concussion, then I had to stay awake.

But I didn't.

TWENTY ONE

Dear Diary,

There was a magnificent fire that appeared before my eyes, roaring like a locomotive furnace as my lids fluttered open and a flood of intense pain exploded between my ears. The demolition crew had arrived inside my head toting jackhammers. Even my forehead was throbbing so hard I could feel each pulsation.

I had somehow stumbled to the couch and passed out and now I could see the daylight streaming in from behind the curtains. The entire room stank of Katherine's blood—of what was left of her rotting body.

He was either not awake, and I was, or it dawned on me that perhaps he was indeed conscious and just faking that he wasn't. I decided the answer lay in the process of making sure he was awake.

I searched inside my kit and didn't find what I was looking for, so I went into the kitchen and pulled open drawers. Bingo.

And when I came back out striking the first match from the box and walked right up to him and he never reacted, I realized he hadn't been conscious at all during any of this time.

I dropped the first lit match on the top of his scalp where I'd pulled out his hair. With an angry hiss, it went out the moment it hit his sweat-soaked head. I refused to give up. With a second match I tried again, getting it to land dead smack in the middle of his part, right on the pasty white surface of his scalp.

He stirred, still deep within the temporary hibernation of unconsciousness. I grew impatient, my head still throbbing like mad from before, so I snatched three matches from inside the box and, once lit, held them under Whiney- Ass' chin.

His head snapped back as if on a wire and he glared at me with eyes so comically wide that I couldn't help but burst out laughing.

"What the fuck is wrong with you? What in the holy fuck is fucking wrong with you!" he tried screaming, at least that's what it sounded like he was trying to say with that sock wedged into his mouth. But it was those eyes, those crazy-ass wider-than-manhole-cover eyes of his that set me to laughing again.

"I have the understanding of what it takes to make someone else feel pain," I told him. "Like with all the stupid shit you say to people without even knowing. Or maybe you do know and you do it anyway. What does that say about you?"

His upper lip started quivering.

I leaned down so I could look him in the eye. " Where I can find Eddy."

He shook his head at me, though obviously afraid of what I might do to him.

"You don't want to tell me?"

Again he signaled no.

"It's the reason I came over here," I told him, making sure he could see enough of my face to know I was telling the absolute truth. "But while I'm here, I also figured we could talk about this job you offered me," I called out as I made my way over to his desk.

"What do I want?" I replied to a question not even asked. "Let's start with a few things, including the perks."

I gripped the ball point Bic I'd taken from a cup full pens and held it in front of his face. I clicked the button over and over. Point out. Point in. Point out. Point in.

Finally, I decided on point out.

Very slowly, I pushed the end closer to his face and he strained his neck trying to pull away, his pupils darting from me to the tip of the pen, then back to me. And as the ballpoint brushed the outer edge of his right side eyelashes, I could see him panic. His face flushed and turned red, the muscles along his throat tensed up like thick cables. He squeezed his eyelid shut as I pressed the point of the pen against it.

"I want six weeks paid vacation a year," I told him and I could hear him make a sound that, at least to my ears, implied that wouldn't be possible.

And as I grabbed the back of his head, I could feel the brief resistance of his right eyeball as I pushed into it from outside of his closed lid with the pen. Briefly, I wondered which would give first, but the answer came as I felt it burst, leaking ocular fluid from under the lid just moments before the pen drove through the skin into the socket.

It was then that Whiney-Ass began to go into convulsions, which I at first thought I could control by turning the pen, but I was wrong. His brain had reacted as if struck by lightning and he shook so hard against the duct tape restraining him that I thought for a moment he'd get free again.

I grabbed him by the throat. "You need to tell me how I can find Eddie so I can stop hurting you now," I whispered into his ear as if we were lovers. "Just give me where he is. I just want talk with him. I have some questions."

And finally I could see that I had broken him because he began to sob uncontrollably.

Why it took this long was beyond me.

I reached into his pocket and pulled out his phone (or did I find it and turn it off before? I couldn't remember for sure, though I seem to recall something along these lines.)

"Why'd you hold out?" I asked pulling the balled up sock from his mouth again.

"He's my younger brother," he finally gasped, choking on a mouthful of swallowed tears.

At first, I stopped dead. But when I thought about it, something made perfect sense. Suddenly, I was imagining their phone conversations—Whiney-Ass reporting back on every single movement I made during the day, every single thing I consumed (soda, lunch, cake). Their huddled whispers used to describe every single detail, real or imagined as they planned their next move for me.

I flipped open his phone. On the small square screen was a photo of Katherine squinching up her face in some kind of reaction to what could only be a joke. Given what I knew of the phone's owner, I could only guess it had something to do with the phrase "pull my finger".

After getting into his phone directory, I couldn't believe how many entries were in there.

Joe Shipmann. Kevin and Marcy Omura. Helen DeKiesel.

"You're one popular motherfucker," I told him, still amazed at the sheer number of names I waded through just to get to the entry for his brother. I found myself shouting as I jammed the gag back into his mouth.

"How does someone as utterly annoying as you have so many friends?"

Rob Rezkowski. Erica Galvan. Tom and Cindy Adele.

And there it was. One word. Eddie. It had been spelled differently than I had thought.

Whiney-Ass sobbed, tears running down his cheek along with the mess that had been his ruined eyeball.

"Shut up," I told him. I slapped him across the face as hard as I could and the force of the blow traveling up my arm shot waves of intense pain rocketing through my head. "Stop crying or I'm going to kill your brother," I lied. I was going to kill him anyway. Both of them. There was just no need for him to know that yet.

And I looked down at my hands as I chose Eddie's number and dialed. They were shaking.

As it rang, I could feel my body filling with rage, like a vessel flooding from the output of a garden hose.

The voice that answered brimmed with a sense of the expected, most likely from having identified the source of the caller ID tag.

"Hey, man," it chimed, sounding so unlike anything I had had heard before.

When I didn't respond. I heard him say, "Hello?"

"Where's Eddy?" I barked into the mouthpiece.

"I'm Eddie, who the fuck is this?" he growled back full of indignance. "Where's Jimmy?"

He sounded young. Too young.

I snapped the phone shut and grabbed the front of Whiney-Ass' shirt. Without even considering the safety of my fingers, I reached into his mouth and pulled the sock out. He drew a deep breath of air into his lungs.

"How old is your brother?" I growled at him.

"Sixteen," he said, coughing. "He's only sixteen."

I opened the phone again. This time I looked at the area code of the number I had just dialed.

"937!" I shouted. "Where the fuck is that?"

"Ohio," he said in between sobs. "Hillsboro. What are you doing? He's only in high school. What do you want with him?"

I did the math in my head. His brother was almost twenty years younger.

"My father's second marriage," he said, reading my mind. "I send them money to help out."

I could have cared less if he was sending them cholera. My anger exploded suddenly, and I threw the phone against the wall, smashing it into a million pieces. I unleashed a sidekick to Whiney-Ass' chest and the wet snap of what could only be his ribs breaking filled the air. Backwards, he flew in the chair and I heard his head smack against the hardwood floor. At first he lay there, unmoving and I thought the blow to his noggin had killed him.

I looked close, at first thinking blood was pooling underneath his head, but when I blinked, it wasn't there and he began moaning. Low at first, working into a dull wail that grew louder with each passing second. I could see him moving back and forth slightly, tears streaming from his eyes.

Here he was, Jim Maddox, a.k.a. Whiney-Ass, arguably the single most annoying person I knew, laying blinded and hurt terribly because of my savage attack. His busted arm twisted, pinned at some grotesque angle underneath his chair.

I had suffocated his girlfriend to death to get information that eventually led me nowhere.

And as I gazed down on Whiney-Ass I felt nothing.

I wasn't even enjoying it at all.

"I fucked up," I told him. "Your brother wasn't the guy I was looking for."

His Eddie was not my Eddy. My Eddy was still out there.

"I'm sorry for whatever I did to you," he whimpered though I could barely make out what he was saying. Then with more effort. "Please help me." I could feel his good hand reach out to me, squeeze my upper arm, then let go.

"Okay," I told him. I went and retrieved my bag and took out the box cutter. I kneeled back down and began slicing through the tape I had wound around his torso, lashing him to the chair.

"I want to let you go," I told him grabbing him by his good arm and lifting him up. But before he was able to get his two feet squared on the floor, I bent slightly at the knees and swept him up over my shoulder. I turned toward the staircase as he shouted and his shattered arm flopped uselessly against my back. Quickly I dashed up to the second floor, putting his feet down at the edge of the steps. What followed was not a shove but Jim letting go as the momentum of his body pulled him downward. He left my fingers, not with force but instead slipped through them like sand.

And it hadn't been meant to end up that way, so there was a slight moment of disappointment as he tumbled backward, bashing his head hard on an upper middle step and collapsing all the way to the floor in a heap.

Slowly, I descended thinking over and over again how I had finally enjoyed the sight of his helpless face and pinwheeling arms as he fell down the steps, my emotions finally breaking through like rays of light on a cloudy day.

There he lay, twisted and crumpled, his legs both facing almost ninety degrees perpendicular to his torso. I could tell right away that his spine had snapped just above the hip.

Somehow, shockingly, he was still alive. I could see Jim's body going into tremors. Kneeling down next to him, I put my ear to his mouth to listen. His breathing was shallow and there was a soft clicking noise coming from his throat. I lifted him off the floor, slung him over my shoulder and climbed the stairs again, feeling the bones in his mostly limp body grinding unnaturally against each other.

At the top of the steps, I tried to get him to stand to no avail, so finally I just gave him a very satisfying shove down the staircase. His top half folded backwards over his bottom half at the spot where his spine was busted and he banged against the walls and railing the whole way down like a human pinball.

There was no doubt this time he was dead. His glassy eyes staring upwards at a ceiling he could no longer see. I thought about the fact that, as far as I knew, no killer in recorded history has used a push down the stairs as their M.O. for multiple homicides. I could be the first if I so chose.

I didn't even look back as I left.

The real Eddy was still out there. I was going to locate him. He would find out what I did to Whiney-Ass Jim and it would stand as a warning to him.

Behind the wheel, I suddenly felt ravenous. The day had faded to late afternoon and I realized I hadn't eaten anything in almost 24 hours. I needed protein and caffeine.

And a cigarette. I found half an open pack in the glove box.

As I lit it, I thought of the word "glove" and it dawned on me that I hadn't worn any at all at Jim's house.

I didn't care.

Moments later, I found myself turning into the parking lot of the chicken place. The thought of tearing into the hot flesh of a roasted thigh or breast, letting the clear juices run from my lips was so appealing. The salty vegetables, the starchy side orders.

Hot mac and cheese, buttery mashed potatoes.

When I entered, to my surprise, there she was, Rio, behind the counter in her tight-fitting uniform.

Her face looked like that of an angel. The way her blond mane shone in the light, the angle of her cheekbone. My heart leapt in my chest. From within, I could feel the emotions I had kept buried. I could feel the lustful stirrings inside of me as my eyes locked on the soft curves of her body. It sounds like such storybook nonsense, but it felt like I was drifting across the floor on a cloud.

My ears grew silent and those around the register parted like the sea.

"Are you okay? Should I call an ambulance?" a short man next to me asked in a low whisper. And suddenly, I could sense a connection between Rio and I as she gazed up at me. In the moment she stood there slack-jawed before she could utter a word, I had to tell her.

"I think I love you," I said.

At least that's what I believe came out of my mouth because it was really the shriek let loos from her trembling mouth that brought me back into full consciousness. The fog around me lifted instantly and I could feel my feet landing on the ground with a resounding thud.

As I looked down at myself I finally noticed the mostly-dried blood covering my hands and arms, the crimson stains spattered all over the front of my shirt.

Rio's screaming echoed louder. "Stop it!" I yelled at her, feeling terrible for my outburst. Then as I could sense the eyes of everyone inside the restaurant fall upon me, I turned and fled, getting into my car and driving away.

Inside me was a burning desire to talk to someone, bubbling like pot on a stove. There were words inside my throat that I needed to share. I thought about calling Miss Corn-fed at the office, then changed my mind. Instead, I turned the car onto the freeway and drove to Thomas J. Bonney's grave.

"What's happening?" I asked him as I knelt before his headstone. I thought of him there, six feet below in the peace of slumber eternal. I thought of the chemicals they poison your body with during embalming, to slow the rotting of your flesh. What's the point in preserving a corpse if it's in the ground? Why not let it decompose? Whatever happened to ashes to ashes, dust to dust? Are we that greedy that we have to try and exist forever?

There felt like a presence behind me, and when I turned I could sense her eyes on me. It took me a while to realize who she was. This time, she didn't speak. This time, she didn't bum a cigarette.

But this time I could see her in her true marbleized form, standing watch atop a small granite foundation. Her stone hand was cold to the touch. Her eyes, sculpted to mimic some kind of somber contemplation, gazing out toward the trees.

This time I spoke, the same words she had said to me at Thomas J. Bonney's internment.

"Funny how you never really miss someone until they're dead."

I sped back to my place, grabbed clothes, my emergency cash and my journal before taking off.

As I sit in this motel room, chain-smoking my last few cigarettes, I have been trying to call Eddy, but every time I redial the one number I have for him, I get a message that it's disconnected. If he is watching me, he has to know I'm trying to reach him.

My hands hurt; I can barely hold this pen anymore in my cramped fingers. I want to try to document as much as I can because I honestly don't know what I will remember in the morning or how clear it will be in my mind. I don't know if I will get another chance to write.

If this is the end, then goodbye.

Dear Diary,

I can't sleep. My body wants what the mind cannot have.

There is a feeling in my head of this intense pressure between my ears. I know now it is impairing my judgement, my ability to concentrate.

I decided I needed a dose of reality. I needed to see my Jennie Bomb. Her energy is so positive and loving. If I had a dose of the GFE, I could remember what it was that I was doing. Why my work is so important.

I needed the touch of her hands on my body and the feeling of my tongue on her soft, supple flesh.

I needed to smell her on my fingers.

We march like zombies each and every day through the valley of life. Our jobs and superficial relationships are some kind of walking death. Most of us are just marking time until the moment the end finally embraces us and takes us away from all the needless mental and emotional anguish we bring upon ourselves.

I needed to feel alive again.

I got in the car and began to dial. It took two calls to her answering service within the span of an hour to get a call back. I told her I was coming into town and I had to see her. She was apologetic.

"Honey, I'm all booked up," she said. For once, it didn't anger me to hear that. I didn't care who else was fucking her. I just needed to see her.

Finally, I told her I'd triple her usual rate. She told me she'd call me back. For fifteen agonizing minutes, I tried not to think of the chance she'd say she couldn't do it, or possibly not even call back at all.

I sat in my car by the side of the highway, flipping through the mall girl photos in my phone, thinking what it would be like to pin one of these fifteen-year-old whores to the wall while I push her knees apart, clamp my hand over her mouth and ram my cock into her while she begs me to fuck her tight little snatch. I climaxed hard into a clean fast food napkin.

Dear Diary,

Eddy called me five minutes ago. If he had any idea of what I did at Jim's house, he gave no indication.

"You need to hurry up and get here right now," he said in a whisper. "I can't talk."

"What are you talking about?" I asked. "Where's here?"

He told me to hold on and I could hear him cover the mouthpiece momentarily before returning to the conversation.

"Just come now," he whispered. "You need to see what I've done."

TWENTY TWO

Dear Diary,

Out of nowhere in the summer of 1997, a twenty-seven year old multiple killer named Andrew Cunanan became the headline of every newspaper and tabloid around the world.

Time, Newsweek, The National Enquirer.

Within the span of mere days he had gone from complete obscurity, a clean cut, good-looking fellow known only by his few friends, to a celebrity with international fame and notoriety.

Hard Copy, Dateline, Sixty Minutes.

Some Hollywood stars spend millions of dollars on publicists who can't do that.

All Andrew Cunanan had to do was kill someone famous.

There is so much for me to tell about what has happened over the past couple of days. So little time.

The drive to Las Vegas took nearly five hours. That's a lot of time to think about things. That's all there was to do. Think.

I had seen van with windows black as night driving behind me that one time. How do I know it was Eddy?

I've received e-mails from him. But how do I know where they really came from? I deleted all of them soon after reading to keep them secret for his sake and mine. I think back and it gives me pause.

What did I really read? What did I really see?

How do you prove something is real when the only place you can find it is in your mind?

Those phone calls.

Glenn Campbell's *Witchita Lineman* came on at nearly the same time on two separate stations, so I turned off the radio.

I followed the directions I'd been given. I turned down the cul-de-sac, looking at all these suburban homes piled on top of each other, appearing almost identical with their white stucco and red barrel tile roofs.

At the end of the street was the house. I pulled into the driveway next to the green Prius.

Andrew Cunanan was born during the Summer of Love, August of 1969 to be exact, in an upper class suburb of San Diego. The youngest of four, Andrew Cunanan was highly intelligent, handsome and possessed what was often described by his teachers as a photographic memory.

By the age of six, at his mother's urging, he had already read the Bible cover to cover.

In high school, his flamboyant personality came out, as did his sexuality. According to classmates, he once arrived at a school dance wearing a tight-fitting red patent leather jumpsuit that had been purchased for him by his older male date.

His senior yearbook lists him as having been voted "Least Likely to be Forgotten".

As I entered the bedroom. I saw him, Eddy, dressed in black pants, black shoes and wearing a black windbreaker. He was leaning over the body, slashing at it with short, deliberate overhand strokes. His gloved hands were covered with blood. Her organs had been removed and placed neatly on the floor by the foot of the bed, her intestines pulled out from her guts and wrapped once around a bedpost as if my Jenny Bomb had been a horse to be hitched to a rail.

Even with the knife wounds and her eyes gouged out, I would have recognized her anywhere. My mind flashed to the last time I had been with her. Her mouth on me, my hands on her body. The feel of her warm inner thighs against the skin of the palms of my hands as I deeply thrusted inside of her.

Above the stench of her blood and guts, I could still glean a whiff of her perfume.

And I wanted to cry.

By the early 1990s, Andrew Cunanan had become a fixture in the San Francisco gay scene, often going by the assumed identity of Navy Lt. Commander Cummings in order to impress those he was trying to bed. It was said he had become notorious for bouncing from one older boyfriend to the other in what was often labeled as relationships of convenience since it was these same older men who footed the bill for his rent and lavish lifestyle. One boyfriend had even bought him a brand new Infiniti sedan.

But in 1996, something went terribly wrong. After being dumped by his latest boyfriend and benefactor, Cunanan fell into a deep depression, allowing himself to go to seed.

In the months to follow, Cunanan would slink back to his old haunts, overweight and intoxicated, only to find that his old friends and acquaintances wanted nothing to do with him in this state.

In April of 1997, Andrew Cunanan decided to fly to Minnesota to reconnect with an old boyfriend named David Madson, the only man he ever loved. Cunanan called his credit card company, to whom he was already deeply in debt, and used his beguiling charm to convince them to extend his limit so that he could buy a first-class one-way plane ticket.

What happened once he arrived is unclear. Cunanan apparently convinced another old friend named Jeffery Trail to let him crash on his couch. On April 27th he and Trail went to Madson's trendy loft apartment where neighbors overheard a fight break out.

Two days later, police searching Madson's apartment found Jeffery Trail's body rolled up inside a carpet. Nearly three-dozen steel hammer blows to the face and head had rendered him nearly unrecognizable.

Just about forty-eight hours afterwards, Cunanan drove to a lake a half hour outside of Minneapolis where he shot

Madson several times in the face with the .40 caliber handgun he had stolen from Jeffery Trail.

Within the week, Andrew Cunanan had made it to Chicago in Madson's red Jeep. Finding himself in desperate need of cash, he somehow gained entrance to the home of seventy-two year-old real estate mogul Lee Miglin. After robbing Miglin, Cunanan stabbed him repeatedly with pruning shears before opening the old man's throat with a gardening saw.

There is no evidence Cunanan ever knew Miglin before.

Before I could utter a single word, Eddy looked up at me. From behind dark sunglasses, he glared into my eyes for just a moment before speaking.

"They're on the way," he whispered. "They have orders to shoot on sight."

"You aren't real," I said.

"You'd like to think that wouldn't you? If that were true, then it means you have no control over your own actions, that you have created me in your mind as a coping mechanism. We don't have time for your neuroses right now."

Andrew Cunanan next headed east in Miglin's 1994 Green Lexus. On Friday, May 9th, he shot and killed a cemetery caretaker William Resse in Pennsville, New Jersey.

After making the one-thousand-mile drive to Miami, on May 12th, Cunanan holed up in a dive called the Normandy Plaza Hotel, whiling away the next couple of days with TV, takeout pizza and S&M pornography.

"Why?" I asked Eddy, unable to peel my stunned gaze from the mutilated form of the gentlest creature I've ever known. "Why?"

"Do you still want to get the Interstate Slasher?"

"Of course."

"I can help you do it."

"What the fuck are you talking about? What was all of this?" I gestured to the bed. To everything.

"You've completely lost your track, so I'm going to get you back on the right path. What we know is the man you're looking for was in jail for the four years he didn't kill. Now he's gone to ground. But he had a cellmate who's still inside. We can put you in that cell. You're gonna find out who he knows, where he went, where he could be hiding. And while you're in there, you'll do some other little clean-up jobs for us as well."

On the morning of July 14th, Cunanan, dressed in a simple white shirt and grey slacks strode down Ocean Drive, past the world famous art deco hotels of trendy South Beach, past the cafes where movie stars and fashion models put themselves on display in the guise of having lunch. He then approached fifty-one year old celebrity designer Gianni Versace outside of his 35 million dollar beachfront palazzo and shot him twice in the head with the same .40 caliber gun used to kill Madson and Reese.

Shortly thereafter, police located Reese's red pickup truck, inside which they found a U.S. passport for one Andrew Phillip Cunanan.

I stared back blankly. My entire body felt numb. Grief, disbelief, anger. It was all there.

"Yes, I used you. Welcome to the real world. And of course, I intended for you to get arrested. But it's for a higher purpose. You know that saying about breaking a few eggs, right?"

I felt like I had to sit down.

"You have a gift to do what it is that you do. I've seen lots of guys like you."

"You do this a lot?"

"We keep our eyes on guys like you. People with your interests and abilities. And when the time is right, we test them and redirect their focus to meet our goals and help make the world a slightly better place."

The room was spinning. My head was pounding.

"We don't have time. Decide now. You work for me. You do what I say and I'll make sure you're taken care of.

"Who?—"

"—Don't ask me who I work for. The answer is not something I think you're ready to handle." He paused. "How would you like to get your hands on some real scuzzballs. How'd you like to find the killer of Jon Benet Ramsey?"

The manhunt for Andrew Cunanan has often been called the largest in Florida's history. As police and federal agents from all over the country searched high and low for him (and reports of sightings poured into hotlines from coast to coast), Cunanan's face graced every single newspaper and television channel around the globe.

And still he eluded capture for 11 days.

On July 25th, on a houseboat tied up in a small marina just a few miles from South Beach, a seventy-year-old caretaker discovered evidence of an intruder on board. As he went to call police, the air behind him filled with the crack of a single gunshot.

In the boat's main cabin, laying face up on the forward berth, police found Cunanan clad in only his underwear. He had put the barrel of the .40 caliber handgun in his mouth and pulled the trigger.

"Look on the bright side," Eddy said pulling a pack of cigarettes from his pocket and offering me one. He had read my mind. "California prisons are all smoke-free. You'll finally get a chance to quit," he said, lighting my cigarette.

"I'll be in touch," he told me, then turned and walked toward the door, stopping briefly. "If it's any consolation, I believe your little diversion in the newspaper did get his attention."

I stood by the bedroom window looking out onto the street out front waiting to watch Eddy leave, but the door I heard close inside the house came from the back. All I could see in the cul-de-sac were a pair of kids riding red bicycles, chasing each other, playing cops and robbers.

Dear Diary,

I have begun this entry with my hand bleeding all over the back of someone else's notebook, which is almost such an unbearable violation of their private space that I am having trouble holding this pen. There isn't much time so I will write quickly and probably forget a few things along the way.

This is what I remember:

As my eyes opened this morning, I had forgotten where I was. There were spiders on the ceiling above the bed. Many of them. I hadn't noticed them in the dark when I checked in. In the light of day, I could now see the water damage in the corner. The peeling paint. The broken chair.

What was I to expect? I had left Vegas and driven until I couldn't keep my eyes open anymore.

At least the room had a bed. I turned on the TV. Apparently they found the bodies of Jim and Katherine. The reporter on scene used the word "grisly" three times. She also mentioned that police claim my prints were all over the house.

Nothing about my Jennie Bomb. Not yet.

They have not made the hunt for me public. Not yet.

I did ten situps, and then began to think about what may be hiding in the shag rug of this no-tell motel and got the willies. I decided instead to go for a walk.

It was early; I slipped behind the wheel and drove through the town of 29 Palms to Joshua Tree Park. I paid the ten bucks to get in.

I drove with the windows down, the hot desert air blowing through my unwashed hair until I got to a point on the map the ranger at the front gate had mentioned.

Once I closed the car door, I was overwhelmed by the complete silence around me. The only thing I could hear was the slight breeze sliding past my ears. The dry terrain and smooth rocks everywhere, worn down thousands of years ago by flowing rivers now gone, made me feel like I had left the earth for someplace else.

I walked up the road a bit, staring at the humongous boulder across from me, the one called Skull Rock. It indeed did bear a striking similarity to the front of a human skull. What kind of petrified giant had this been?

My mind opened. I felt my head swimming in a sea of such uncertainty. I thought of everything that had happened, of all the good I have done.

But do I trust Eddy? That I couldn't work out.

I drove back to the motel, unsure of what exactly my little nature hike had accomplished. I needed some aspirin. I needed a shower.

While gassing up my car, I noticed a diner across the street. My stomach rumbled. I couldn't remember the last thing I had eaten.

The smell of warm food hit my senses like a blow to the face. Immediately, I wanted a plate full of everything.

Hotcakes, French toast, oatmeal, country-fried steak.

I sat at the counter and asked for a Denver omelette. Hash browns. English muffin. Large orange juice.

I should have taken closer notice to the way the waitress refused to look at me while I was ordering.

When the two cops first entered, I didn't see them; I felt them, like a cold breeze on the back of my neck. I turned just in time to see the hostess point right at me. What happened next is a blur. I shattered my water glass on the counter, the sudden crack bringing the whole place to a swift silence. Holding the big broken shard to the neck of my waitress, I grabbed her by the hair and dragged her into the kitchen. I told them what I'd do to her if they tried to come in after me.

I think something in the tone of my voice made them realize I was serious. Even though the cook apparently didn't speak much English, he knew enough to take off running. Or maybe he didn't have a green card.

She saw it before I did and the movement of the waitress' head toward the big chopping knife on the counter alerted me to it. I tossed the jagged hunk of glass aside and that's when I noticed for the first time all the blood streaming from the large cut in my palm.

I shoved the waitress to the red tile floor as I snatched up the knife by its well-worn white plastic handle. On the counter was a towel that I wrapped around my hand. I yelled out to remind the cops to stay out of the kitchen unless they wanted her blood on their hands.

When really, what I had was my blood on my hands. I had to figure out a way to buy time.

The waitress began sobbing loudly.

"You're the one on the TV," I could hear her say. At least that's what I think it was.

I gazed down at her face; her mascara ran down her cheeks like lines of wet sooty tears. She was young but didn't look it. She looked cheap and easy, like the kind of broad who wouldn't think there was anything wrong with sucking your dick while alternating between drags on a cigarette.

I had to point the knife at her to get to shut up, which she did only briefly while I bolted the back door.

I sat on the floor with my back to the counter and lined metal tubs across the service window so they couldn't see me, so nobody could get a clear shot. At least with a hostage, I could keep them at bay for a little while.

Though she wasn't so cooperative. Even as I held the knife to her throat, I could sense she was about to scream. That kind of distraction would bring them in here guns blazing. That I didn't want. So I locked her inside the walk-in freezer for safe keeping.

Outside, I could hear the place filling up with cops. Someone pushed a cell phone through the door with a broom handle. It rang almost instantly.

"I'm Bill, what's your name?" asked the man with the soft voice. In the movies and TV, the hostage negotiator is no-bullshit, brusque. This guy sounded like he was taking my order for a floral arrangement.

I laughed. "I think who I am is quite obvious."

"How's Caroline?" he asked. Referring to the waitress by her first name was his way to humanize her in my eyes. It was so obvious.

"Chilling out," I answered.

He wasted no time trying to get inside my head. "Why did you do it?"

I gave him my reasons without hesitation, all of them. "Tito Gomez was a monster. Phil Testaleone was a monster." I reminded him of the terrible crimes they committed.

He then told me neither of those guys did anything wrong.

"What about the teeth marks on the little fingers inside of Phil Testaleone's trophy box?"

"Those dental impressions weren't a match to Phil Testaleone," he said. "They're a match to you."

I was silent. I had let him get inside my head during a momentary lapse of diligence.

"Stop fucking with me!" I howled before throwing the phone against the far wall of the kitchen.

To this day so-called experts debate whether Cunanan was indeed a serial killer or just a spree killer. What will they say about me?

As I sit on the floor and write this all down, it can only be moments before they come in here. I'm ready for whatever happens. I can no longer tell if what burns in my soul is a quest or some kind of possession—if I even have the strength to take the next step.

If I cut myself, what do I feel?

As I sit on the floor and write, I can hear the phone ring.

But not the broken phone now laying in the corner, my cell in my pocket. And I can't believe what I see on the caller ID.

Eddy's number.

I want to answer but I can't, so I just let it ring.

And ring.

And ring.

*****

AUTHOR'S NOTE...

MYN here. I promise the Madman has left the building...
One time, I was in Vegas and just about a half hour after we
had checked in there was a huge fire at one of the big hotels
across from where we were staying. Within minutes, it was all
over the news. In fact, we saw it playing out on a TV screen
above a casino bar.

To say the least, I was dumbstruck.

These being sensitive times the whole thing seemed, well,
suspicious and I'm sure there were a number of folk whose
first knee-jerk reaction when they saw the flames or the news
on television was to think the "T" word.

Me, I was one of them. My initial thought was that I was
somehow watching a moment from "The Doomsday Club".

And why in the world would I ever in a million years
think that some highly-unlikely, totally made up scenario
from one of my crazy books could possibly come to life?

Because just weeks before, a dead body was found in the
same spot where Red gets dumped in "Diary of a Madman".
Are you listening to me? THE EXACT LOCATION. And
yes, it's a real location.

It gets better.

The cops estimated the stiff had been there about three weeks before some L.A. County clean up guys came across it while clearing out leaves.

Which would place it at the scene about 2 weeks after I released the serialized podcast episode in which this similar incident occurs in the book.

Holy shitballs! Was my madman real? Could someone have heard my podcast and used it to get ideas on unwanted corpse disposal?

Yeah, let's not go there. I'm sure it was complete and total coincidence. But I gotta say it did creep me out badly.

The Carl Bishop murder location in the book is a real location I've visited to walk my dog several times. I have even found bones there. Small animal bones, most likely the leavings of a coyote's snack but bones nonetheless.

And there is this one big creepy dumpster.

I have no idea how long ago this construction site was abandoned but they did leave behind a 30 cubic yard dumpster that is full of...

...well, what I couldn't tell you because honestly, I'm just a bit too freaked out to actually climb up into it and check underneath all of the left over PVC pipe, broken concrete and the other construction junk that's been tossed inside.

But I have peeked around it thinking there's a chance I could find a human hand stretched out in some kind of desperate rigor mortis.

--Shudder--

I've often described "Diary of a Madman" as a splatter-punk symphony of extreme graphic sex and violence wrapped up in a tight noir narrative about loss of self. Some people have heard about the book and thought "serial killer who kills other serial killers" and have compared it to "Dexter". Honestly, I had never read or seen any of the "Dexter" series before writing this. I've since become a fan of the TV show (well, most of the TV show... the overly-clichéd love story between Battista and LaGuerta makes me want to throw up in my own mouth) but the real inspiration for this book was The Juice himself.

O.J. Simpson.

Right around the time news of his "If I Did It" book came out my flaming douchebag of a boss at that time, sent me a bootlegged early version of the manuscript and wanted to do an unofficial, unauthorized audio book of it before it came out.

I was game, my employer wanted it. I couldn't believe the insanity of what I was reading... the self-justification O.J. had served up in defense of murder made me nauseated. I knew that I didn't want to editorialize the already-inflammatory content but I still wanted to imply some kind of guilt so I did that in the way I performed the voice. I read it in the monotone of a cold-blooded killer—dispassionate, emotionally detached from reality.

It worked great. But then a day or so later the news hit that the rights to the manuscript were being awarded to the family of Simpson's murdered wife as part of the unpaid civil judgment against him. Ripping off an asshole like O.J. would be one thing but we couldn't do that to the victim's family. I scrapped the project.

But damn, I did like the way the read came out. I wanted to do something with that voice.

And so, during one of my dog walks to that very same body-dump location, I came up with the idea for "Diary of a Madman". From there, as it often does when I write, the book just took on a life of its own.

Though the book stands by itself as a singular piece of fiction, some of you who have followed my twisted fiction over the years now know that "Diary of a Madman" is actually book two of the "Angel of Death Chronicles", coming after "Badlands" and just before "Angel of Death".

These universes are all connected.

How so? Well that, dear friends, is something that you'll just have to stick around to find out but I promise you it won't be a boring ride. So please stay tuned... and if you enjoyed this book, please tell your friends about it. Tweet, post it on Facebook. Spread the word.

Best,
MYN

ABOUT THE AUTHOR

Mark Yoshimoto Nemcoff is a bestselling and award-winning author living in Los Angeles who has been known to occasionally moonlight as a TV host, voice-over artist and rock journalist. A professional composer of music for television for many years, opportunity knocked and transformed him into a screen/TV writer and author featured on "Access Hollywood." Then a podcast recorded in his car became a weeknightly drive-time radio show on Sirius Sateillite Radio. This led to a handsome feature in Playboy Magazine that compared Mark to Howard Stern and Jon Stewart.

Mark can be reached at: MYN@WordSushi.com

Twitter.com/MYN
Facebook.com/MYNBooks

If you enjoyed this book, please tell your friends.
-MYN

BOOKS BY MARK YOSHIMOTO NEMCOFF

NON-FICTION:
- The Killing of Osama Bin Laden: How the Mission to Hunt Down a Terrorist Mastermind was Accomplished
- Where's My F*cking Latte? (And Other Stories About Being an Assistant in Hollywood)
- Go Forth and Kick Some Ass (Be the Hero of Your Own Life Story)
- Pacific Coast Hellway Presents - Pissed Off: Is Better Than Being Pissed On

FICTION:
- Diary of a Madman
- The Doomsday Club
- The Art of Surfacing
- Number One with a Bullet
- Shadow Falls: Badlands
- Shadow Falls: Angel of Death
- Killing My Boss
- Transistor Rodeo

SPECIAL THANKS

Much, much thanks goes out to the wonderful podcast audience who first discovered this book and to those of you out there who have followed my crazy shit over the years.

And for those of you above-mentioned lunatics, I have something very special for you...

AND NOW A SPECIAL PREVIEW OF
INFINITY

PROLOGUE

Forever, the din arose, bringing with it the inevitable.

The red Mercedes continued in reckless haste, bounding with insanity across the tripled northbound lanes of Pacific Coast Highway. Ian Augustine refused to lose them. When his targets accelerated to seventy, he punched the gas of his black BMW 3-Series, closing the distance. Pedal down, his slalom swerve between a white Suburban and beater pick-up truck gained him the slightest bit of ground.

The tingle in the back of his head was hot. *I've got you*, Ian thought. *Today you're going back to Hell.*

Beach mansions whizzed by on the left. To the right, there was nowhere to go but up, into the Santa Monica Mountains. The man driving the Mercedes stole glances at his wife's panicked face.

Turning off on any of those side roads would make it easier to be caught. The light off-season traffic was in their favor. With luck, they would lose their pursuer by putting cars between him and them.

Ian pulled a Sig Sauer P245 from the glove box. Full clip. Ready for close encounters. He snapped off the safety and dropped the barrel down into the cup holder.

Not getting away this time.

They had given him the slip before. It had been one of the hottest days of summer and he had tracked them to a farm outside of Ithaca, New York. The pair had worked the entire East Coast as psychotherapists convincing simple, everyday people that they been the victims of childhood molestation by members of the clergy.

Over forty-one lawsuits had been brought.

As expert witnesses for the plaintiffs, they would testify to the horrors their patients continued to suffer because of the cruelty of these so-called "men of faith."

Nightmares. Nervous Breakdowns. Depression and Anxiety.

"Authority and power enable predators such as these to coerce the victim—in these cases children—into doing things for dominance, sexual gratification, or, mostly, both," Dr. Rinier would iterate to terrified juries while he cleaned his glasses.

Addiction. Dissociative States. Gastrointestinal Distress.

The symptoms were myriad. The punishment should fit the crime.

The settlements bankrupted the church—but it was mostly the suicides the doctor and his wife were after.

One monsignor, guilty only of steering troubled boys in the right direction, cut his wrists with a sliver of broken mirror. Another had swallowed enough drain cleaner to liquefy his insides until he died screaming.

The two or three priests who had actually been guilty of something had also taken their lives. "The more the merrier," Dr. Rinier told his wife, Caina, as they toasted their success.

In the cellar of their farmhouse, they told Ian, at gunpoint, about the things that would happen to his family. Even his parents, both many years in the grave, would be dug up, their bodies defiled. "I'll sip soup out of your mother's skull," hissed Rinier.

In the ensuing scuffle, the couple escaped. It was weeks before Ian located them again.

There was no way these two were escaping this time.

The two cars shared abandon. The red Mercedes blew through a red light; Ian followed.

Lanes were wide open. Their speedometers made it to eighty. The Mercedes throttled up fast. Ian accelerated in turn, gaining.

Shoot them at close range. Get away. Dump the car. Leave town.

Just like he'd been trained. Just like he'd done countless times before in the name of the Church of Infinity.

Ahead, the three lanes became two. Bottleneck. Ian knew he could get them.

Until the red Mercedes swerved into oncoming traffic. Head-on into the southbound lanes.

"Sumbitch!" Ian smashed his palm against the steering wheel in frustration. Grabbing the shifter, he switched the BMW from automatic to manual transmission and dropped it from fifth gear to fourth. The car rocketed ahead, revving up into the red as it crossed the double yellow line.

He barely missed the black Honda blaring its horn at him. He swerved back into the northbound lanes to avoid a school bus.

The red Mercedes was getting away.

For a second time, he jumped the dividing line. A heart-stopping near miss with a minivan cost the red Mercedes speed and Ian was in position again. He downshifted once more, the engine screaming as it redlined. Within seconds he was right on their tail.

If he could catch the back corner of their bumper, he could pit maneuver them off the road.

Just a little bit more; a little further.

He cut left at the same time as his prey and they blocked his advance. Ian juked right, but they matched him move for move.

A bread truck came directly toward them, the driver hitting his horn intermittently, as if delivering frantic bursts of Morse code. The two speeding cars evaded to the left.

Seeing his opening, Ian cranked the wheel right, entering the space the bread truck had just passed through. The Mercedes slowed momentarily because of a green SUV coming toward it. Ian knew this was a small miracle.

In mere seconds he was next to the Mercedes, his Sig Sauer pointed out his driver side window.

As if time had slowed to a crawl, Ian could clearly see both driver and passenger—an old man and the woman, their expressions full of terror as they spotted his gun.

Once he pulled the trigger and the bullets ripped into their mortal bodies, Ian finally caught a glimpse of their true faces.

To his horror, they looked very human.

The dead man slumped over the wheel. The Mercedes drifted out of control, first smashing door-to-door into Ian's BMW before ricocheting head first into a guardrail. The sheer force of the crash lifted the back right wheel of the Mercedes off the ground. The rest of the car followed as it traveled up and over at an angle, hitting the rocks below as it fell.

Desperately, Ian fought against the steering wheel of his car to regain control before it fishtailed too far and followed the Mercedes.

They weren't demons. In Ian's mind, he saw their faces again and could not escape the thought that he made a terrible mistake. *What have I done?*

It was the sudden and distinct blast of an air horn that brought his eyes forward—to the 18-wheeler barreling down upon him. The truck grill's grinning face bloomed larger and larger. The accelerated rate of closure caused its unchanging gape to fill the windshield with the visage of death.

The 18-wheeler's air horn quickly blanketed the air. Ian felt it shake him from head to toe. Momentarily, his gaze jerked upward, away from the oncoming grill of the truck, to the rearview mirror.

Those dark blue orbs staring back did not correspond with his physiological responses—the hurricane swell buffeting his mind; the tense feeling in his chest; white knuckles on the steering wheel.

Instantly, he knew the moment to pull away had come and gone; he was past the point of no return. Even if he could turn the wheel and change his trajectory, something told him it wouldn't make a difference.

And he braced for impact.

Want to read more?
INFINITY a novel by Mark Yoshimoto Nemcoff
Wordsushi.com